Lust

and

Lemonade

Renaissance

Cover art and design by Caroline Frechette. Layout by Caroline Fréchette. Edited by Evelyn Cimesa, Caroline Fréchette, and Victoria Martin.

Legal deposit, Library and Archives Canada, May 2017.

Paperback ISBN: 978-1-987963-24-3
Ebook ISBN 978-1-987963-25-0

Renaissance Press
http://renaissancebookpress.com
info@renaissancebookpress.com

Lust

and

~ A Novel ~

Jamieson Wolf

For Michael and Dava

Chapter One

"So which one of you fuckers is going to pay for this beer?" Blaine turned and faced them.

Nancy, the delightful one. He was also incredibly feminine. Fruity, if you will. "I can't," he said. "I just picked up a new MAC foundation and the new Britney CD." Nancy shrugged as if this should be common knowledge. "I'm fresh out."

Blaine looked at Chuck. He was always out for a good time. Blaine knew he'd have cash on him. But Chuck shook his head. "Sorry man." He grinned. "But I got me some K."

"What the hell is K?" Blaine asked.

"It's the new thing, apparently," Chuck said. He looked around and quietly took out a little baggie. "Gives you a full-on body buzz."

"It's cat tranquilizer," Mike said.

Blaine gagged. "*Cat* tranquilizer?" Blaine took a sip of his beer to clear the awful taste in his mouth. "Why do you *do* that to yourself?" Chuck was always trying out new drugs and never turned down an opportunity to experiment. He also had more money than God and the Pope put together. If you're going to live the lifestyle of an upper class queen, you gotta have the money.

"Well, it's all right," Mike said. "But it makes you feel really groggy afterwards. I tried some with a guy I met down at The Cabin." The Cabin was a happening scene for the young to the middle-aged. It was also rumoured to have one of the best cruising bathrooms in the city.

"We did it right there in the bathroom, fucked me in one of the toilet stalls." Mike smiled. "William got so huffy when I told him about it last night." William was Mike's partner. They explored what would be termed as an 'open relationship.' Or, since neither slept with the other, you could call it a 'very open relationship'.

"You didn't let him fuck you bareback, did you?" Nancy simpered. "A lady has to protect oneself, you hear?"

Chuck laughed. "I don't see no ladies here."

Nancy admired his nail polish. "Well, speak for yourself, but I *am* a lady." Nancy snapped his fingers. "Oh *hell* yeah." He turned to face Mike. "So did you? Fuck him bareback?"

"No," he said, laughing. "He had a condom with him, pulled it out of his pants pocket."

Blaine laughed. "No one is *that* prepared."

"Tell me about it," Mike said. "I turned to him and asked him 'Have you done this before?'" He laughed. "Still though, good ride. My ribs hurt a little today."

Blaine sighed and took another swallow of beer. "Too much information." He reached for a cigarette off the table and lit it. Inhaled. "You are such a fuckwit." Blaine sighed again. "So is no one going to help me out here?"

He seemed to be the designated beer wench. Every single fucking time we go out, he thought. I mean, I really don't mind. Sometimes you have to pay to have friends. Money makes things easier.

Blaine sighed. *Right, keep telling yourself that*, he thought. Blaine knew the answer to his question and took out his wallet. "You guys are such fucking assholes, you know that?"

"What's up with you today anyways?" Mike asked. He ran a finger through his spiked hair to make sure every blond lock was in place. You must look presentable at all times, after all. "You've been all cunt-y lately." He reached for one of Blaine's cigarettes and lit one for himself.

Blaine shrugged. "Just out of it I guess." He shrugged again. "I miss David."

Nancy sighed. "If I have to listen to another story about how much you miss that nasty man, I'm going to go straight." He shook a finger at Blaine. "You mind me! I will not suffer through another summer with you talking about how he treated you." He took a sip of his Mai Tai. "He demeaned you," he said. "*There*, I've said it."

"Take it easy, Mona," Chuck said. "Leave the boy alone. He's just going through a dry spell, is all."

"Just leave it alone," Blaine said, turning away. "I don't want to talk about it."

"Maybe you have to," Nancy said. "It's been six months."

"I know how long it's been."

"There's no law against dating, is there?" he tried.

Blaine shook his head. "No."

"Then why are you still alone?" he asked. Nancy was on a roll tonight. Once in a while, he latched on to something and never let go until you'd heard what he had to say. Some people thought he was a flashy femme queer, but he was more than that. He was intelligent and a brightness was there. Say what you will about him though, the fag knew about fashion.

He reached out and touched Blaine's hand. "We just don't like seeing you so lonely, Blaine," Nancy told his friend. "You're gorgeous; you just have to get back into the game, put yourself back on the market."

"Maybe I want more than that," Blaine said. "I've seen what's on the market."

Nancy shook his head. "Well, honey, what else is there? It's all about wham, bam, thank you, Stan. Tenderness doesn't exist."

Chuck snorted. "Says the man who believes in 'true love.'"

3

The way he said it, they knew the quotation marks were in place. You could almost see them in the air. "I'll believe it when I see it."

"True love exists," Nancy said. "You can't disprove that. You *can* prove that there is too much hardness in this city." He took another sip of his Mai Tai and reached for a cigarette. "It's a fact of life."

Blaine shrugged. "Well maybe I want something more than that," he whispered. He didn't think that Nancy had heard him speak, but he did.

"Oh, honey?" Nancy smiled. "You want love, don't you?" He took a drag of his cigarette. "Well, then let me tell you something." He pointed a finger at Blaine who blinked in surprise at its fierceness. "True love can't be found."

Nancy stubbed out his cigarette. "It finds you."

Blaine shrugged and took out his wallet to pay for the beer.

Chapter Two

Poppy wondered if tonight was *the* night.

She put a hand protectively around her womb and held it there, hoping. River Moon Falls looked disturbing with a knife.

Poppy looked at her, really looked at her. She tried to see if the River Moon Falls she had fallen in love with still existed. She didn't think so. Stepping forward, Poppy spoke quietly. "What are you making?"

River Moon Falls (formerly Connie Collins from Nebraska) turned and glared at her. "You know what those bastards did today?"

Poppy shook her head and wondered who had earned the mighty wrath of River Moon Falls this time. Didn't people know that you just never, ever took on a lesbian lawyer? Those gals would scalp you.

Poppy knew that River Moon Falls' job as a civil defence attorney stressed her out. She just wished that River Moon Falls wasn't quite so vocal about it. She cringed inside, waiting for the tirade to start; she could feel it coming. She even had a line to say: "What did they do?" Poppy asked.

There, she had said it. Now River Moon Falls would continue for another forty to forty-five minutes. Poppy sighed. It was what she always did, *every* day, upon her return from work. She let River Moon Falls talk instead of having a conversation. Most of their relationship had consisted of monologues instead of dialogues.

"Well." River turned, cutting knife in hand. Poppy saw the gleam of it and then spied the half-massacred chicken on the counter. River Moon Falls always cooked while she was angry, which probably had a lot to do with her lack of skills as a chef.

"I went in this morning to find all of them in a meeting." She held up the knife as if in salute. "A meeting!" she emphasized. "Without me! Those men were keeping me out of the loop."

"Oh, I don't think it was that," Poppy said. But she might as well not have spoken. River Moon Falls continued unheeded.

"They were meeting about one of my accounts. All of them, standing there with their dicks out, pissing on each other."

"What kind of meeting were they having?" Poppy asked.

"It wasn't that kind of meeting. I was using a figure of speech. I mean, just because those men have penises, they think they can strut around like kings of the world. Look at me, I have a penis!" River Moon Falls stuck the knife down near her crotch, point sticking out like some lethal phallus.

"Don't you think you're overreacting?"

"No, I don't think so. I don't think so at all. I mean, have you ever seen one of those things? Dicks? They look like dead chicken necks." River Moon Falls turned her head and seemed to notice only now what she was making.

With a decisive chop, she severed the chicken neck and slipped it off the cutting board into the trash. "If only it were that easy."

Poppy made some half-hearted reply and turned away from her, going into the living room. Sitting on the couch, she turned on the television, not seeing anything.

She absent-mindedly patted her stomach and thought about what to do.

Chapter Three

Mike let himself into the apartment and shut the door behind him. With any luck, William wouldn't be home.

Lady Luck wasn't with Mike that evening.

As soon as he had taken off his shoes and headed to the kitchen, he heard William coming. His husband stopped at the doorway and propped himself there. "Have a good night?"

Mike sighed. Why was it always the same thing? Did everything have to be a pattern in life? "Yeah."

"Were you out with the boys?"

Mike shrugged out of his coat. "If by 'the boys', you mean Nancy, Blaine, and Chuck, yes. I was out with the boys."

"No one else?"

Mike looked at William's gorgeous face and his dark gold eyes. He breathed in and out and reminded himself that he cared for this man before he lost his patience. "No one else."

He took a jug of water out of the fridge and poured himself a glass, letting the silence stretch between them. He knew that eventually William would say something. That he would speak.

"Where were you at lunchtime?" he asked.

Mike sighed again. His lover was not one for subtlety. He always cut right to the punch. "I was out. With a friend."

William blinked as if Mike had slapped him. Perhaps he hadn't expected Mike to be so honest. "Did you fuck him?"

Mike smirked. "What's it to you?"

William's face showed a moment of rage. "We had a deal."

Mike held up a hand. "Yeah, a deal you seem to be forgetting."

William stepped back, went and got a cigarette out of his

pack. "What do you mean?" His voice was quiet.

"You were the one who wanted an open marriage," Mike said. He figured if he said the words quickly, he could get this part of the evening over with. "You wanted me, but with no strings attached. We could play with whoever we wanted; we just had to let the other person know afterwards." Mike turned away from him. "That was the deal."

"I didn't think you'd go out fucking everyone you saw," William fired at him. "That wasn't part of the deal."

"It wouldn't be so bad if you went out and found a trick every once in a while," Mike said. "Instead of being cooped up in this place all day."

William looked at Mike as if Mike had spat at him. "Fine then, maybe I will."

Mike huffed and butted out his cigarette. "Fine."

"Fine!" William said. He turned away from Mike and went into the bathroom. Mike could hear the water running.

"Bitch," Mike said.

He looked around, wondering where he had left his weed last.

Chapter Four

Nancy didn't mind being alone.

He knew that Blaine would be going home to his empty apartment, Mike would go home to fight with Will, and Chuck would be out on the town, looking for the next lay. But Nancy was content to sit inside The Crosstown Bar and people-watch.

It was his favourite activity. He watched people in bars, walking along the streets, sitting at patios. And he'd make up stories about them. It helped pass the time. It helped get out his frustrations. Some people painted, some made music. He made up stories.

He knew that his friends thought he was a flaming queen, but he didn't mind. As long as he could people-watch, he was all right. He wondered though if he had any talent for writing.

He'd been feeling the itch to write his stories down.

He reached for a cigarette, lit it, and motioned to the bartender for another beer. He would have one more before leaving; he would be able to people-watch for a bit then go home to watch some porn.

What else was a girl to do with a free weeknight?

The bartender came over with another beer and set the glass down in front of Nancy, who was pulling his wallet out of his purse. The bartender waved his hand. "Don't worry about it," he said. "Free of charge."

Nancy looked at the bartender, really looked at him. He had shaggy blond hair that made him look like a surfer dude, large blue eyes, and a mouth that was currently smiling, showing off bright, white teeth. "Free of charge?" Nancy said. "Like I don't have to pay for it?"

The bartender shook his head. "No, it's on me." He held out his hand. "My name's Devon."

Nancy smiled. "How butch." He held out his hand. "Name's Nancy."

Devon blinked in surprise. "Nancy? Really?"

"Yes." He shrugged, took a drag off his cigarette. "My parents wanted a girl."

"Why didn't they pick a different name when they saw that you were a boy?" Devon looked at Nancy, raked his eyes over his body. Nancy felt himself blush.

"They were so sure they were going to have a girl, they didn't think of any other names. So they named me Nancy."

"Holy shit, that's strange."

Nancy waited a few seconds and then burst out laughing. "Sorry, sorry, I couldn't help myself. I was yanking your chain."

Devon smiled, his blue eyes dancing. "I wondered if you were putting me on."

Nancy held out his hand again and Devon took it. "My real name is Clarence."

Devon looked at him again, those blue eyes scrutinizing his face. "You don't look like a Clarence."

"See? Nancy's better."

"Are you doing anything later?" Devon asked.

"Define 'later.'"

"Well, I get off in about an hour. Did you want to go for a coffee or something?"

"Why, Devon," Nancy said jokingly. "Are you asking me out on a date?"

Devon smiled wider, flashing his white teeth. "I think I am."

"Then I'm accepting. Should I meet you here?"

Devon nodded. "I'll meet you out front."

He leaned forward and kissed Nancy softly on the lips. When he pulled back, Nancy felt as if the room were spinning. He watched Devon walk back towards the back of the bar and, for once, felt that all was right with the world.

Who needed people-watching when you had a hot date?

Chapter Five

"I worry about you, Blaine."

Blaine's grandmother was making him pink lemonade. She had made some for him during every visit since he had come out of the closet. He didn't mind; it was her way of showing acceptance. "There's nothing to worry about, Nana."

"Pssh! How long has it been since you've been on a date?"

"A few months."

"A few months! Exactly! You can't let David ruin you forever, honey; he's not the only man in the world, you know."

"I want someone I can build a life with, Nana."

"Fine, but that doesn't stop you from getting a bit of cock."

"Nan!"

"What? It's true! Just because you have your sights set on true love doesn't mean you have to live like a monk in the meantime. David tried to ruin you, Blaine. But now you're free!"

"If he was so awful, why did he dump me? Why didn't I dump him?"

"Because you're both idiots. He was cheating on you and went for greener pastures."

"I'm not an idiot, Nana."

"Then prove it! Stop letting him control you!"

"It's not that easy to meet men."

"Blaine, it's only a bit of rumple foreskin, you can get that in a bar, can't you?"

"I don't just want a quick fuck," he sighed. "That's all that's out there, all other men want."

She brought the pink lemonade to the table and sat across from him. She patted his hand and squeezed it gently. "You still want love."

"Yes, I guess I do."

"Do you think you need to change what you want?"

"No, Nana, I can't. I've let every guy change me and I won't change what I want."

"So, you want love, but you're too afraid to go out and look for it?"

Blaine nodded. "Silly, huh?"

"It's not silly. You have to get out there though, honey; you won't meet anyone sitting at home feeling sorry for yourself. But I have an idea."

"Oh?" Blaine didn't like the way his grandmother was smiling. It never boded well.

"I've found you a job," she said. "You start tomorrow."

"Nan, I've already got a job!"

"Yes, yes, your call centre work. So engaging! No, this is something you will do every Monday, Wednesday, and Friday. You'll be volunteering at the GLBTQ Library down on Third. You'll ask for Ms. Robinson."

"Well, I highly doubt she'd let me volunteer without talking to me first."

"Of course she would, she's a good friend of mine. We get our hair done together every other Tuesday. She's a lovely woman! Tomorrow is Friday; you'll report after work. She's expecting you."

She patted his hand again and smiled at him. "It'll be fine honey. Now drink your lemonade before it gets warm. It'll taste like a cup of warm piss."

Chapter Six

Chuck slapped down two twenty-dollar bills.

The Caveman Room charged a lot to get in, but they were the cleanest. He had never walked on cold cum on the floor or found the rooms dirty and gross. If you wanted a clean playground, you had to pay the money.

Joe was behind the window. He took Chuck's money and slid a towel and a room key toward him. "Third time this week. Someone's really fucking horny."

Chuck took in Joe's blond hair and cheek bones, his chiseled good looks. He wanted him in the worst way, often jerking off while thinking of him. "Don't you ever play? There's nothing wrong with coming here a lot, I pay my money, don't I?"

"Sure you do, but there's more than this, you know? I used to play around a lot but stopped. It was all empty, you know?"

"Thanks for the life lesson."

"Whatever, man, just being friendly. You're in room ten; have a good night."

Chuck took his towel and made his way to the locker room. He saw a few guys getting ready, and one man was wearing a towel, looking around himself apprehensively. Chuck nodded to them and made his way further down the bay of lockers. Finding an empty row, he chose a locker and started getting undressed.

When he was just pulling off his pants, he heard footsteps. Looking up, Chuck saw the guy in the towel. He was gorgeous, with a muscled chest covered in a light dusting of hair. He had striking blue green eyes with flecks of grey, but it was his smile that made Chuck want to kiss him all over.

"Hey? I'm sorry to bother you."

"Not a bother at all. What can I do for you?"

"The truth is, I've never been to a place like this. It's all a little overwhelming."

"You've never been to a bathhouse before? You don't look like you need one." Chuck looked him up and down. "You should have no trouble meeting men."

The guy actually blushed and it made Chuck melt just a little bit more. "I'm shy. I have trouble meeting men in crowds or at bars."

"Well, now you met one. Chuck Jones." He held out his hand.

"Sebastian Carmichael. Nice to meet you, Chuck."

"How can you be here if you're shy?"

Sebastian pulled back his towel and Chuck saw he was wearing a jock strap underneath. "Easy. Protect the assets."

Chuck laughed aloud. He couldn't remember the last time he had actually had a conversation in the bathhouse. Normally he just got sucked off in the sauna or fucked a guy in his room. This was nice. Unexpected, but nice.

"Want to come back to my room? We can get to know each other better there."

Sebastian blushed an even deeper shade of red. "Actually, I was thinking we could go to dinner instead. Would that be okay? If it'll sweeten the deal, I'll let you suck my cock afterwards. I don't know if I can do anything with an audience."

Laughing again, Chuck was unprepared for Sebastian's next move. He leaned in quickly and took Chuck's mouth with his own.

Chuck expected the kiss to be sensual; what he didn't expect was the intense warmth that rushed into his chest the moment their lips made contact, filling his entire body with heat and befuddling his head. Breaking away from the kiss, he looked at Sebastian again, really looked at him

"Where did you want to go for dinner?" he asked.

Chapter Seven

There was a knock at his door.

Blaine opened it to find Poppy standing there holding a bottle of champagne. "Hey honey, what's the occasion?"

"I need to celebrate."

"What about River?"

"She's playing at being Connie again tonight."

"Gone back to her bull dyke roots, has she?"

"She goes on about being in touch with her inner Goddess, but she's really just an angry ball-breaker. Are you going to invite me in?"

"Sure, honey, sorry. How did you know I'd be home?"

"You're always home. You don't ever go out." Poppy waltzed in, closing the door behind her. "You're my one constant."

"Fuck you very much."

"Well honey, it's true. You never go out, you're always at home. What do you do all evening, anyway?"

"I write some of my poems and then read. I clean up around here, have a cup of tea, and go to bed."

Poppy yawned theatrically. "Oh, what, sorry sweet cheeks, I fell asleep from utter boredom. What were you saying?"

She sat on the couch in his living room, crossing her legs. "Anyway, get some glasses. I have news and I want to share."

Blaine looked at the bottle. "You know I can't drink white wine or champagne. Gives me a headache."

"It won't matter Blaine. It's sparkling."

Blaine raised an eyebrow. "Yes, it usually is."

"No, you dumbass, it's non-alcoholic."

"Poppy, you haven't had a non-alcoholic drink in over ten

years."

"I know," she said. Poppy reached down and rubbed her belly. "I have to, now."

Blaine sat down; actually, he pretty much flopped down beside her. "Honey, are you...? Are you really...?"

Smiling broadly, her eyes big and bright like stars, Poppy held out her hands above her head. "I'm pregnant!"

Blaine was stunned silent for about a second. "Oh my God! Does River know? No, of course not, she's not here, and I thought you were a lesbian anyway, you're a lesbian, I mean you are a lesbian, right?"

Poppy waited a beat before responding and gave Blaine a pout. "Okay, got all that out of your system?"

"Yes, I think so."

"Good, so are you happy for me?"

"Of course I am! But Poppy, I mean...shit!"

She shrugged her shoulders. "I know, right?"

"How did it happen?"

"Seriously, Blaine? It's not like this is the Immaculate Conception. You know how people do this, right? Or has it been that long since you've gotten laid?"

"It hasn't been that long."

"Long enough if you've forgotten how it's done."

"Okay, okay, I know how it's done."

"Good. So do you want to meet him?"

"The father? Why would I want to meet him?"

"Because he's gay, too! Isn't that great? I get a baby and you get a date. I mean, what are the odds?"

"You have to fill me in here, because I'm missing something."

Sighing, Poppy lay back on the couch and shrugged again. "We met at a bar. We were both bitching about our partners.

18

It was really all very innocent. We just wanted to feel love again and confirm our sexuality. He's still gay and I'm still a lesbian. He's actually very nice."

"What are you talking about, Poppy? You can't set me up with the father of your baby."

"Sure I can, and I did. Hey, there's no reason we can't both get something out of this. I've gotten you a date for this Saturday. How awesome is that?"

"I can't just go meet a person I don't know!"

"Where's your sense of adventure? Sure you can! Honey, you have to get out of this apartment. It's been months since you've gone out and done something! Besides, he's going to be my baby daddy. You have to meet him. What's the harm?"

"First my grandmother, and now you."

"Now 'me' what?"

"She said the same thing. Got me a job volunteering at the Gay Lesbian Bisexual Transgender Queer library."

"Blaine, that's fabulous! I always loved your grandmother, great minds think alike." She picked up the bottle of sparkling champagne and held it out to him. "Now get some glasses, honey. If you let this warm up before you drink it, it'll taste like piss."

Chapter Eight

Mike sat there, wanting to say something but not knowing what. So he remained silent. All that could be heard was the clink of their spoons against their bowls and the clatter of their drinking glasses on the glass table top.

Every once in a while, William would make an angry sound, like an enraged rhino, and he would slam his spoon down and rustle the paper as if wanting to choke the life out of it. Finally, Mike could stand it no longer.

He threw his own spoon down with a clatter and picked up his pack of cigarettes. He took one out and lit it.

"No smoking at the table."

Mike responded by blowing out a large plume of smoke. "So how about you tell me what's wrong?"

William shrugged. "Nothing's wrong."

"Please! You've been angry and sulking for a week or more. If I didn't know any better, I'd say you were a woman on her period."

"Well, I could be, you never look at me down there, so how are you to know?"

"What the fuck does that mean?"

"You never want to touch me, never want to fuck me; you always go out and screw other men, as if I'm too disgusting for you."

"What the fuck are you talking about?" Mike stubbed out his smoke and lit another one despite William's angry glare in its direction. "We have an open marriage for fuck's sake."

"I know that."

"You were the one who wanted the open marriage, you wanted to have a companion but sleep with other people;

'playing the field', you called it."

"I know I did."

"So what's the fucking problem?"

"I'm in love with you."

"You mean you love me. I'm aware, I was at the wedding, too, you know."

"No, you're not listening. I'm in love with you, have been for some time; it came upon me without me knowing. I went to bed one night and I was fine, but woke up absolutely and totally in love with you."

Mike snorted. "But you were the one who wanted the open marriage!"

"I know."

"You wanted to fuck and suck other people, you told me!"

"I know I did."

"And *now* you love me? We've never once talked about love!"

"Hey, I'm not happy about it either."

"Then change your heart back, change it, please."

"I can't. I've never loved someone like I love you. I can't just shut it off. A heart isn't like a faucet. It's on or it's off and right now, it's gushing."

Mike was silent for a moment before he spoke again. "So what do we do now?"

"I don't know. I have an idea, but I have to know, how do you feel about me? Do you love me at all? I have to know."

Mike pushed his chair back and stood. He made his way to the bedroom but, right before he left the dining room, he turned back to William.

"I've always loved you," he said and left the room as quickly as he could.

Chapter Nine

The date last night had gone well. Nancy didn't know when he'd had a nicer time with a man that didn't involve a quick and dirty fuck.

They had just gone out for coffee. With the way Devon looked, Nancy half expected Maxwell's to be this seedy little bar, kind of like The Cabin, only grungier, less hip. That was all right; he could blend in if he had to, he could work it in a crowd just fine.

However, Maxwell's turned out to be this lovely little coffee house. It had a yellow awning that was bright like the sun. It had large picture windows done in dark red leather and trimmed with gold along every edge.

Nancy had felt as if he had walked into a dream. Not only because he had misjudged Devon, but also because he was completely charmed. They had found a table in the back of the place. A small candle was flickering in the centre of the table. Nancy had taken a seat so that he could see the door. Hey, a girl never knew when she'd have to make a quick exit.

"You look like you're a little shell-shocked."

"I'll be honest, I expected another bar. Muscle boys and half-naked girls grinding. That kind of thing."

"I look at that kind of thing all day. When I'm off work, I just want to be normal."

Nancy picked up a menu and began flipping through it. "Well, colour-me-impressed. Do you know the last time a man took me out for a date in a place that wasn't a bar? I don't remember the last time I went somewhere that didn't serve non-alcoholic drinks."

"Try it, you'll like it." Devon smiled at him.

Nancy wasn't sure if Devon was talking about the coffee or referring to himself, but Nancy found himself further charmed. They talked long into the evening, only pausing for sips of coffee.

When the shop was getting ready to close around midnight, Devon reached across the table and took Nancy's hand. "I've never met anyone like you."

Nancy felt his cheeks redden. He could feel the heat coming from Devon's hand, and it sent a thrill running through him. "Well, this is different."

"What is?"

"Finding a connection instead of a quick fuck."

"Not so bad, is it?"

"No," Nancy's voice came out in a whisper. "No, it's not at all."

Later, while lying in bed, Nancy had wondered if there really was such a thing as true love at first sight. Not that he would go and give his whole heart to Devon: he wasn't that stupid. However, he believed in the notion of it.

When he woke, Nancy went to the gym. It was where he did his best thinking and a girl had to stay in shape. Plus, it never hurt to sweat it out a bit, and he didn't like the gay, fucking saunas. All those nasty men looking at you, whether you were straight or gay or in between. At least at a gym, every guy pretended to be straight, even if they weren't.

All that Nancy had concluded after an hour-long yoga class was that he wanted to see him again. No, it wasn't the deep realization that one usually had after a yoga class, but it was enough.

Nancy was coming out of the gym when his cell chirped at him. He looked at the number and smiled. It was Devon. He clicked his phone and put it to his ear. "Well, speak of the

Devil."

"Why, were you speaking about me to someone?"

There was a hardness in his voice that took Nancy aback for a moment. "No, honey, I was just thinking of you, that's all. It's just a figure of speech."

"Oh!" His breath of relief was loud, even over the phone. "Oh, okay. What are you doing this afternoon?"

"Well, most normal people have to work in an hour or so. By which I mean me. But I can be persuaded to take a lunch somewhere"

"Won't your boss mind?"

"Honey, I am my own boss. I'm a graphic designer. I make my own hours."

"Awesome. Where should I pick you up?"

"Oh my, are you asking me out on another date?"

"That would be a yes."

Nancy gave Devon his address and hung up the phone with a grin still on his face. The grin didn't last long, however. He couldn't help wondering at Devon's grim voice or the sound of utter relief when he had clarified what he had meant. That stopped the warm shiver that had been running through Nancy as he answered the phone. Now he was just cold.

Nancy didn't know what was up, but something was wrong. And a girl didn't need any Spidey sense to know that.

Chapter Ten

"Thank you for calling, how may I help you today?"

Blaine was pretty sure this was hell. He was almost positive of it, in fact. Call centre work wasn't glamourous, it didn't pay well, and Blaine was really beginning to dislike the human race. It was good in theory, but not in practice; at least, not the part that he talked to.

"Yeah, I'd like my credit card back."

"What do you mean, Ma'am?"

"I gave y'all my credit card when you asked for it and I want it back."

"I don't understand, Ma'am. Why do you want your credit card back?"

"Well, when y'all asked for my payment, to surf in the internet web, I put my credit card in the slot that looks like a bank teller machines. Now, it won't process my payment and won't give me my card back! I want it back!"

Blaine thought for a moment and something clicked inside his head. "Ma'am, do you mean the disc drive? Did you insert your credit card in the disc drive?"

"Yeah, the slot thing. How else are you going to read my numbers?"

Putting his head in his hands, careful of the headset, Blaine took a deep breath. "Ma'am, you just had to type your numbers in with the keyboard."

"Well, it didn't *tell* me to do that. Why didn't it say to type the numbers in? It just said to *enter* them! How am I supposed to get on the interweb? My granddaughter wants to Skyper with me! I can't do that now!"

His heart going out to the woman, who had obviously

never been near a computer before, Blaine took another deep breath. "You can find your number on past statements, Ma'am. We only sell the Internet; you'll have to take your computer to a repairman to get your card out, though."

"Oh, really? Can I really still get on? She wants to talk to me tonight and I still have to install this web cam. Did you know she'll be able to see me over the interweb! Isn't that amazing?"

"Yes, Ma'am. It is."

"You can call me Shirley. I'm Ms. Godrough to most people, but you can call me Shirley. Will you help me with the instilling?" She took a frustrated sigh. "I'm just not very good at this."

"It's okay, Shirley. I'll stay on the phone with you and tell you what to do."

"You're an angel. You're going to make someone a fine husband someday. Your mother must have raised you right."

"I'd like to think so, Ma'am."

He talked to her for the better part of three hours, helping her first install the internet and then her web camera software. She was overjoyed.

"It all works! Oh, I can't thank you enough Blaine! I'll be able to talk to my granddaughter! Oh, it'll be such a treat to see her; she's been in Europe for three weeks! It's been so long, I'm used to spoiling Emily once a week!"

"Well, she'll be happy to see you, Shirley."

"You're an angel of the Internet, Blaine. Thank you."

He said goodbye and hung up his headset. He loved calls like that one. At first, he had started not to bother with his calls in order to get fired. When no one came to see him to talk about his quotas, he decided to take calls again. It was fucking boring doing nothing all day.

26

Blaine had decided to resume taking calls, but with a twist: when a call came through from someone that was genuinely upset, he took the time to help them. No one ever came to talk to him about proper call length or up-selling. So he continued helping those he could.

His Nan thought it was just call centre work. He thought of it as giving back.

His shift over, Blaine grabbed his coat and closed down his computer. He only hoped he could give back as much at the GLBTQ Library.

Chapter Eleven

Chuck sat across from Sebastian and wondered how this had happened.

He had a different guy every night. Always fuck a new hole, that was his motto. Now here he was, sitting in the local greasy spoon, having gone out for dinner with him last night, then drinks, and now breakfast, and they still hadn't fucked.

Chuck was still flabbergasted at the fact that they hadn't fucked yet. Yeah, they'd made out a lot, but still nothing R rated. It bothered him that he was okay with that.

Sebastian laughed and nudged him on the arm. "You okay, Chuck?"

"Yeah, yeah, I'm fine."

"I've been talking to you for five minutes and you didn't say a thing. You had this lost look on your face."

"Sorry, I was lost in thought."

"About what?"

"Oh, no, it's silly."

"Try me."

"Nah, it's going to make me sound like a pig."

"Men are pigs, Chuck. What's that short for anyway?"

"That's something else you'll laugh at."

"So tell me the first one then."

"Really? Okay, um, well. I can't remember the last time I spent so much time with a guy and we weren't already fucking or sucking by now. Actually, it would probably be over with by now."

"And you'd be on the prowl for the night ahead?"

Chuck shrugged. "Pretty much, yeah."

"Does that bother you? That we haven't had sex, yet?"

"It should. It's why I went to the bathhouse. It's my usual MO."

"So why are you still here?"

"Because I like you."

His honesty shocked him. Chuck blushed, and he tried to cover the moment with a sip of water. He put his glass on the table and looked up to find Sebastian looking at him with a wide smile.

"I like you, too, Chuck. That wasn't so hard, was it?"

His blush deepened. "No." The word came out in a whisper of a breath. "No, it wasn't."

"Good, so then telling me what Chuck is short for?"

"It's short for Charlie. My dad named me, but my mom gave me the nickname, after Charlie Brown. Peppermint Patty always calls him Chuck."

"That's cute, Charlie Brown. Thank you for telling me."

When Sebastian smiled at him, Chuck thought something was wrong with his stomach. It was like there were butterflies inside of it. "You're welcome."

"Good, now that's settled. Can I take you back to my place and fuck you now?"

Chuck had taken a sip of his water just as Sebastian had asked this, so he choked on it and ended up spitting some out in shock. "What was that?"

"You heard me. You told me something really honest before, probably the most honest any guy has been with me ever. I want to show you my thanks somehow." He smiled with his perfect white teeth that melted a little bit of Chuck's wall.

When Sebastian reached across the table and grabbed his hand, Chuck realized it was the most public display of affection any guy had shown him. He looked at Sebastian, really took him in, and realized that he might already love this man.

"I'd like that. I'd like that very much."

Chapter Twelve

Looking at his watch, Nancy tried to pretend that he wasn't waiting for Devon, that he wasn't almost pacing or wondering why Devon hadn't called him back. Lunch had passed a few hours ago and there had been no word from him.

Nancy had finished his work day in a slight huff. He hated getting fucking pissy for a fucking guy. He just couldn't stand himself when he did that, then he really did feel like a fucking woman.

It was as if he was on hormones. It happened every fucking time: he met a guy, they hit it off, and they had a few dates and then... nothing. Just a sea of quiet where words should be. Nancy would see the men out and about in bars later, and they wouldn't even look at him.

It had been years since anyone had touched him, or had even wanted to. Flamers put most men off; it was a well-known fact. Nancy had always known this; it was just a fact of life. He wondered if he could work that into a novel or something, maybe a poem. He had all these ideas but never wrote them down.

Maybe he should start. Tell people stories that he made up in his head. Write them down once and for all. He had been thinking of it a lot lately. People had to let their voice out, right? It was all about being heard somehow.

He jumped when he heard the phone ring. He was running for the phone before he stopped himself. A lady didn't want to be out of breath when she answered the phone; however, in his haste to curb his enthusiasm, he tripped over his coffee table.

Landing with a hard thud on the floor, he decided to let

31

the answering machine get it. Fucker Devon could leave a fucking message. In the end, however, his curiosity just got the better of him. Nancy had to hear Devon's voice. However, it wasn't Devon's voice. It was Mike's. "Nancy? You okay? You sound out of breath."

"Just jerking off, bitch, you know how it is."

"No, what's wrong?"

"I fell, asshole."

"Then why did you answer the phone?"

"I thought you were somebody else."

There was a beat of silence before Mike spoke. "Don't tell me you're sitting around your place, waiting for a guy to call you. That's not like you at all, Nance, and you know it. The men should come to you."

"Oh honey, I know. I learnt the hard way. What's up with you?" Nancy sat up and massaged his left foot and leg. He figured if he was going to have a conversation, he might as well get comfortable.

"William told me that he loved me."

"Why is that a big shocker? I was at your commitment ceremony, wasn't I? Didn't I throw flowers at your feet?"

"That was just the ceremony. You know he always wanted to fuck other people"

"Honey, that's why you married him. You wanted Mr. Right and Mr. Right Now. What's the issue?"

"I already told you. William really loves me."

"Oh." Now it was Nancy's turn to be silent. "And what did you tell him?"

"I told him that I'd always loved him."

"Shit honey, that's fantastic!"

"Is it? I mean, my whole fucking world changed this morning. What am I going to do now?"

"Honey, are you for real? I mean really real? Do you hear yourself?"

"I mean, everything is different now. How can we freely love each other after all this time?"

"Okay, you need to fucking snap out of it. Emergency meeting at The Cabin, in twenty minutes."

"Blaine is volunteering at the library."

"Then he can join us later. I need to whack some sense into you. Be there and I'll call Chuck. Twenty minutes and I can talk some fucking sense into you." Nancy hung up the phone.

It seemed a woman's work was never done.

Chapter Thirteen

Blaine looked at the library entrance with some trepidation.

It's not that he was afraid of libraries; in fact, he had spent large portions of his childhood amongst the comfort of books and stories waiting to be read, lands waiting to be discovered.

Libraries had been his sanctuary growing up, his Shangri-La. His safe place.

This would be the first time he worked in one. He wondered if he would be able to do this. Blaine did better hiding from people rather than engaging with them. Well, that would have to change. He thought of Nan, the report she would be expecting from both him and Ms. Robinson.

Taking a deep breath, Blaine walked to the front door and stepped inside. Immediately he was taken back to his youth: shelves and stacks of books, the smell of paper and ink. Unable to help himself, Blaine walked to a shelf and ran his fingers along the spines of the books. The touch was like a talisman and brought him comfort.

"That's something my old heart loves to see," a voice behind him said. "The rapture of books that have yet to be read."

Blaine turned and came face to face with an older woman. She had her hair styled in a short bob, and it was white as snow. Blue eyes like sapphires looked at him merrily and a mouth, done up in a beautiful red, smiled at him.

The woman held out her hand. "I'm Ms. Robinson. You must be Blaine, Cordelia's grandson. Nice to see you're early for your shift, I like people who are early or on time."

"Nan always told me to be early or on time for everything."

"It's a good rule to follow; you don't miss anything that way."

"Yes, Ma'am."

"Oh, please you can do away with all that Ma'am nonsense! Just call me Romilda. Last names are so formal! Now let's get started!" She turned and walked towards the back of the library and Blaine followed. "Now your shifts are every Monday, Wednesday, and Friday from four to seven. You can choose to volunteer more often if you would like. We're quite short-staffed here lately. We need all the help we can get!"

She led Blaine to a small back office with lots of windows. The office was clean and warm, and Blaine was immediately comfortable. Romilda gestured to a seat. Blaine noticed how big her hands were. Then he took in her stature as she moved behind her desk and sat down.

"Clocked me already have you?"

"I'm sorry?"

"It's okay dear boy, if you're not there yet, you soon will be. I was born a man. My name then was Ernest Edwins. I think you'll agree that Romilda Robinson is far better."

Blaine's cheeks flushed. "I didn't, I mean, I wasn't-"

"Oh, it's okay, dear boy. Don't be flustered, though your blush makes you quite fetching. Everyone is safe here and we have an 'open mouth, insert food' policy." She let out a laugh that was like water. "Your grandmother didn't tell me you were so shy!"

He blushed further. "I don't get out a lot."

She raised a finger and wagged it at him. "We'll change that, dear boy. Yes, we will. Now, your duties will include shelving books and helping patrons find the books they want. Sound simple enough? You'll also help with the front desk and checking books out. We let people check out books for two weeks at a time and we don't charge late fees. Takes the joy out of reading if you have to rush through a particularly hard book, don't you think?"

"Yes, Ma'am...Romilda."

She gave him a dazzling smile and let out another short laugh. "You're learning! Good! I'll introduce you to Justin — he'll be the one showing you around. Justin! Come and meet Blaine!"

Blaine heard footsteps and turned around to face the office door, just as the most incredibly handsome man walked into the office.

Chapter Fourteen

Blaine was pretty sure his heart had stopped temporarily. His cheeks flushed and then his heart was off like a racehorse inside his chest. Justin wasn't just handsome. If there was one word to describe him, it would be 'beautiful.' He had black hair that fell to his shoulders in a riot of curls. Soft brown eyes took him in. Justin's jaw was covered in stubble and Blaine found he wanted to run his fingers along it or find out what it was like to kiss him. Justin had thick, beautiful lips and dimples on both cheeks.

Justin held out his hand. "Hi, Blaine. I'm Justin. Justin Black."

Standing quickly, Blaine rubbed his hand on his pants and took Justin's hand. "Nice to meet you," he said.

When they shook hands, warmth filled Blaine. He had never believed in Nancy's insistence that love at first sight existed, but he had to admit that he might've had a point after all. Blaine didn't know if what he was feeling was love or lust; he would have to figure that out later.

"It's nice to meet you, too," Blaine said.

"There's no need to be nervous. I won't bite unless you want me to," Justin said.

"Oh, Justin, you cheeky boy! Now go show Blaine around like a good boy and don't frighten him too much." Romilda turned to Blaine. "I know you'll be very happy here, Blaine. We're so happy to have you."

"Thank you, Romilda."

"Oh, you learn quick. Go out amongst the books, dear boy, and see what they have to tell you." She waved her hands. "Go on now, embrace the future!"

Blaine stood and followed Justin out of the office. Justin tuned to face Blaine. "Your adventure begins." He smiled at him and Blaine's heart skipped a beat.

"Does she always talk like that?"

"Romilda? Yeah, she's pretty awesome. So are you."

"How do you know? You don't even know me yet."

"Yeah, but I want to get to know you. That ought to say something, right?"

Blaine reminded himself to close his mouth and swallow. He hadn't been so instantly attracted to someone in ages. Perhaps ever. Blaine really did have to talk to Nancy and find out if true love, or instant attraction, was actually like this. Even looking at Justin made him dizzy.

"You're awfully quiet. Are you okay?"

Blaine decided that honesty was the best policy. "You make me nervous."

"In a good way?"

Taking a deep breath, Blaine nodded. "Yes."

Justin smiled and Blaine's heart thumped again. "Good, then maybe I can take you out for a drink when our shift is over? I can help you get over your nervousness."

His heart in his throat, Blaine nodded again. "That would be nice."

"We'll just start you off on the front desk today. Do you read a lot?"

"Always have. Books are my friends."

"I feel the same way. Then you should be fine. Just help people find the books they want or find something to read. I'll check on you in an hour."

Blaine nodded and watched him walk away among the shelves and wondered if this was madness. Going out for a drink with a guy he had just met? Well, you had to tear the wall

38

down at some point. He just hoped he was strong enough to do it and take down the whole wall.

Throwing himself into helping the patrons, Blaine didn't even notice his shift end. He helped people find books by Armistead Maupin, Joseph Olshan, and Oscar Wilde. He found that, rather than being nervous, his natural love for books put him at ease and he was soon talking up a storm, suggesting titles to read and sharing his love with others. His voice faltered when Justin came up to him, and Blaine was surprised by how nervous he was.

"You're very good at this. Did you know that when you speak about books, your whole face lights up?"

Blaine tried to calm his breathing. "Thanks. I just love books."

"It shows. I was going to come and get you after an hour, but I had too much fun watching you. You really shine bright, Blaine. Want to go get that drink now?"

Blaine was about to answer when his cell phone rang. He pulled it out and saw Nancy's number on the call display. He answered it. "Hey Nancy, what's up?"

"Emergency, danger, danger! Mike and William are in love with each other and Mike is freaking out! Emergency meeting at The Cabin, now!"

"Oh, but I was just about to go out for a drink, with a guy."

"Oh honey! What's his name? Does he have a big dick?"

"His name is Justin." To Justin he said, "My friend Nancy want to know if you have a big dick?"

Justin grinned. "I've never had any complaints."

"Oh, he sounds dreamy! Bring him along, honey, so we can give him our seal of approval!"

"Nance, I don't know, it was just a drink date and I wanted to get to know him." Justin's grin widened into a smile when he heard this and Blaine swooned a little bit.

"What better way to get to know someone than among friends! Bring him! Be here in five!" With that, Nancy hung up.

"Want to go to The Cabin?"

Chapter Fifteen

Blaine wasn't really sure if this was a good idea.

He had just met Justin and didn't know anything about him, aside from the fact that he wanted to fuck his brains out. That hadn't happened to Blaine since David, and that had lasted only a moment before the trouble began.

It was almost like he was taking Justin to the Lion's Den for a formal interview. He was nervous and agitated. Justin saw his distress and took his hand.

"I'm sure it'll be fine. I can't wait to meet your friends."

"Not quite the first date I had in mind, though. You haven't met my friends yet."

"They're your friends, I'm sure I'll love them."

They were walking down Sunnyside towards The Cabin. The afternoon was turning into the evening. Blaine loved this time of day: everything was the same, but it all changed. It all looked different. It was as if a blanket were being thrown over the world.

"Thank you for doing this."

"Hey." Justin stopped walking and pulled Blaine closer to him. "It's okay. You don't have to be nervous, I can handle myself in a room full of queens. I'm here because I want to be."

When Justin leaned forward to kiss him, Blaine let him and kissed him back. His lips were soft and supple and sent a thrill of electricity through him. Even more startling, Blaine had a small flutter in his stomach. Blaine had assumed the chance to feel that flutter again had died. He pulled back from the kiss with a gasp.

"What's wrong? Did I hurt you?"

Blaine shook his head. "No, no, nothing like that. I

thought something was gone, but it came back, so it's a good thing."

Justin grinned at him and raised his eyebrows. "I don't understand what you mean. You've lost me there."

"Maybe I'll explain it later."

Justin kissed him again, softly this time "I hope you do."

They rounded the corner and found themselves standing in front of The Cabin. Blaine stopped, still holding Justin's hand. "Oh boy."

Justin laughed and kissed him again. "It'll be fine, Blaine. Really."

"Okay, don't say that I didn't warn you."

He opened the door and stepped into the music, half-light, and smell of booze. He saw Nancy wave to him from a table and made his way back, still clutching Justin's hand. Chuck and Mike were there, too. As Blaine and Justin moved closer, they could hear Nancy speaking to Mike. Chuck was nursing a beer.

"I really don't know what the fucking problem is, honey. You have what I spend my life searching for. What's the issue if you fucking love each other? Isn't that wonderful? Isn't that grand? You're freaking out over the greatest gift a person has to give."

"But we've always done the open thing, and to find out that he's loved me all this time..."

"Honey, you've loved him all this time too, open relationship or not. I really don't see what the hang up is."

Nancy turned to Blaine and Justin. "You must be the new guy. So happy that Blaine has met a looker. What's your opinion? What say you, sexy man?"

Chapter Sixteen

Justin squeezed Blaine's hand. Maybe he was a little nervous? Blaine only hoped that he would forgive him for this initiation by fire.

"Well, how long have you been together?"

"Six years," Mike said.

"Have you ever slept with each other?"

"No, we've always gone out and found other men to play with. Then we come home and tell each other about it."

"But you've never tried sleeping with each other?"

"No."

"Are you attracted to him?"

"God, yes, William is so fucking hot."

"Then maybe you should try fucking. Do you even kiss and make out?"

"We did before but not for years."

"Then try that too. If the attraction is there, the rest will take care of itself."

"But everything is different now! It's not the same as it was."

"Love changes. It doesn't stay static and the same thing it always was. It deepens over time, becomes stronger. I think William had a lot of courage to tell you. Do you love him?"

"God yes."

"Then show him."

There was silence between all of them for a moment, punctuated by the sounds of other drinkers and random voices. Nancy looked at Justin and sized him up, letting his eyes rove over all of him. Finally he spoke. "Man, that's deep. You can stay. Tell us all about how you and Blaine met."

Justin moved closer to the group and pulled Blaine with him. "I volunteer at the library where Blaine just started. He's a natural; his knowledge of books is astounding."

Blaine blushed and looked down. "Oh, it's nothing. I just like to read."

Justin reached over and put his fingers under Blain's chin, bringing his head back up. "It's not nothing. You should be proud, not everyone could have thrown themselves into it like you did. Never hide who you are, Blaine."

Nancy's eyes widened. "Shit, honey, are you always so deep like this? I'm getting hot in my boy parts!" He looked at Blaine. "He's a keeper, honey. Don't fuck it up." Turning back to Justin, he held out a finger and wagged it at him. "Don't you hurt him either, or I'll fucking cut you."

"Understood. I wouldn't have it any other way," Justin responded.

"Where's the bartender? I need a drink," Chuck said.

"I don't know where he is, the fucker," Nancy said, but at that moment, Devon came up to the bar.

"Anything to drink, guys?"

"Beer," Chuck said.

"Beer," Blaine said

"Beer," Mike said.

"I'll have a beer please," Justin said.

"I'll have a white wine spritzer, you cocksucker."

There was silence again at the table and Devon gave a sharp look of hurt. "I'll be right back with your drinks."

No one spoke as he left, and Blaine turned to Nancy. "What was all that about?"

"We had a date and then he was supposed to pick me up for lunch. I spent all day today waiting for him and he never showed. Fucker."

"Maybe he had a good reason?" Mike said.

"He should have called. There's such a thing as manners, you know."

"Just ask him what's up, can't hurt."

"I don't want to."

"Yes you do," Blaine said. "I can see it in your face. You looked at him as he left as if you haven't eaten in a week."

"Not true, he's a shit."

"Just talk to him," Justin said. "Find out what happened. If you like him, what's the harm?"

Nancy looked Justin up and down again and smiled. "Well Blaine, this guy sure is a HUGE improvement over your last man. Congratulations!"

"Fuck you," Blaine said.

"No honey, fuck him." He pointed at Justin and grinned.

Chapter Eighteen

Poppy wanted a cigarette.

She knew it was bad, that it would hurt the baby, blah blah blah, so she wouldn't have one. She wouldn't even have a drink. She would eat healthy food and be healthy; her body was Shangri-La.

God, being pregnant was boring.

She took a sip of her decaffeinated coffee (blech) and looking up, saw Justin entering the coffee bar. Poppy smiled when she saw him. "Hey handsome, how are you?"

Justin smiled and pulled her up for a hug. "Never mind me, how are you? How's the little bean?"

"I wish you wouldn't call her that."

"We don't know what gender the baby is yet, do we?"

"No, turkey, I'm only a month into this gig. I'm not going to show for another few months. I just got these pants and I want to have time to wear them."

"You fashion whore. So how've you been? Are you okay?"

"Oh, I'm fine. It's you I want to talk about, though."

"What about?"

"My friend I told you about? I talked to him and he's good for meeting you tomorrow. He's not normally into being set up, but I told him you were awesome."

"Oh, Poppy, you didn't! Why would you do a thing like that?"

"Honey, you're amazing. You've been single for far too long and you're a perfect catch. You need a man to love you."

"Thing is, I already kind of met someone I like. He's a new volunteer at the library and he started last night. We went out to a bar afterwards and he was so fucking hot. He hangs out with this weird crowd of guys, but he's wonderful."

Something clicked in Poppy's head. "The other guys weren't named Nancy, Mike and Chuck were they?"

Justin gave her a look of surprise. "Yeah, they were actually."

"And his name? It's not Blaine, is it?"

Now Justin's mouth dropped open. "It is actually! What are you, psychic? Do you know him? Do you know those guys?"

"You turkey. Those guys are friends of mine but Blaine is the best friend I told you about!" She huffed and crossed her arms. "Here I went through all the trouble of doing a little matchmaking between my two best gays, and you've already fucking met!" She took a sip of her coffee. "This city is too fucking small!"

"That it is. I've said that for years. What are you doing?"

She had taken out her phone. "Calling Blaine....Honey? Stop jerking off and come meet me at Spiga's down the street okay? I'll order you a coffee... okay, see you in a bit." She clicked her phone shut. "There."

"Why did you do that?"

"Well you were supposed to have a date today dumbass, that's why. No point now if you already know each other, is there?"

"I really like him, Poppy. I don't want to fuck this up or frighten him away."

"So don't and he won't."

The door opened and Blaine stepped through it, stopping when he saw Poppy and Justin nestled in the corner of the cafe. Poppy stood and hugged him and gave both of his cheeks a kiss.

"Blaine, my baby daddy Justin. Justin, Blaine. You two

47

play nice now." She gathered her purse.

"Where are you going?" Blaine asked, a note of panic in his voice.

"You two don't need to go on a date this evening now, do you? You can spend the whole day together! Oh, Blaine, I've already ordered, don't worry, you'll like it. Have a good brunch, gentlemen."

Turning from Blaine and Justin's stunned looks, Poppy went to find some ice cream. Matchmaking accomplished.

Chapter Nineteen

Blaine was nervous all of a sudden.

Last night with Justin had been amazing, but he'd had his friends with him. Now it was only them, and he was so nervous he had no idea what to say. Thankfully, Justin spoke first.

"Well, that was nice of her." He took Blaine's hand in his and squeezed it. "There's nothing to be nervous about, Blaine."

Blaine laughed. "It's like you can read my mind."

"The great Justin knows all!"

"Seriously, how did you know I was nervous?"

"I can see it in your face and your breathing has increased. Relax, there's nothing to be nervous about."

"Even the fact that you and Poppy made a baby together?"

"Especially that. It doesn't change how I feel about you."

"You barely know me."

"What I do know of you, I love."

"We've only known each other a short time. What can you possibly know about me?"

Justin sat back and looked at him. "Well, let's see. You know books, so you are obviously intelligent. You've got a kind heart and a good soul, otherwise Poppy would never be friends with you. Your friends are protective of you and loyal, which attests that you're a good friend to them. How am I doing so far?"

Blaine grinned. "Pretty good so far. But you make me nervous."

"Why?"

"Because I like you a lot already. That frightens me."

Justin gestured with his free hand. "Don't be frightened of a connection with someone. We were obviously meant to meet, right?"

"Yes, but it still frightens me."

Justin reached forward with his free hand and stroked Blaine's cheek. "Who hurt you?"

Blaine stared back in shock. "How could you know that someone hurt me?"

"You wear it like a mantle that you're constantly trying to shake off. I can see it in your eyes; they look as big as a deer's would in the focus of headlights. You don't need to worry about me hurting you, Blaine."

"I know. But I'm afraid. It's been so long since I met a man like you, one I'd like to get to know."

"So get to know me, that's part of what connecting with someone's all about right? It's okay to be afraid, but not all the time. I really like you, Blaine. I want to get to know all of you." He squeezed Blaine's hand. "When you want to tell me what happened, you will. In the meantime, we can just get to know each other."

"I thought that's what we were doing."

"Yes, we are. But I was also referring to this."

Justin leaned forward and kissed Blaine. Surprised at first, Blaine found himself giving into the kiss, exploring Justin's mouth with his tongue. He tasted wonderful, and the feel of Justin's tongue exploring his own mouth was intoxicating.

When they broke apart, Blaine was light-headed and slightly dizzy. Never before had he reacted so strongly to a man's kiss. He looked at Justin with new eyes, and the hurt he carried with him lessened a little.

"You okay? I hope you don't mind that I'm into public displays of affection."

"Oh, I'm fine. You just made me hard is all." He blushed at his directness. "Sorry."

"Never apologize for something so wonderful. Did you want to go back to my place after we eat? We could continue the make-out session in private."

Blaine didn't have to think about his answer. "I'd like that. I'd like that very much."

Chapter Twenty

William sat across from him at the breakfast table reading the newspaper. They didn't talk, didn't speak to each other, but the silence was getting to Mike. He decided to take Justin's advice and talk to William, as odd as that notion was.

He put down his spoon and the clatter of metal on ceramic was loud in the quiet. "Um, William?"

William put down his newspaper. "Yes, Michael?"

He looked tired to Mike. He probably didn't sleep well and was tossing and turning. Mike didn't know; he had spent the night at Nancy's. "I think we need to talk."

"You think we do? What is there to talk about?"

"Us, this. Everything."

"What's there to talk about?" William asked again. "You went out last night and played around, not stopping to think how I would feel."

"That's not true. I spent the night with Nancy. I needed some time to myself."

"For what? To fuck him?"

"Fuck Nancy? He's more like a brother than a lover, and you know that."

William had the good grace to look shamefaced. "Sorry, low blow."

"We need to talk about us, William. We can't go on like this. What happened? How did you come to love me when all you wanted was the next fuck?"

William sighed and looked at Mike dead in the eyes. "I don't know how it happened. We'd been together for three years when it started. I looked at you and thought of you as my husband."

"I am your husband, we got married, remember?" He held up his left hand.

"I don't mean like that. That was just a ceremony, just words. But that day, I looked at you and thought "he's my husband." I loved you from that moment on."

"I thought you always loved me."

"Of course I did. I loved you but wasn't totally in love with you. But when that moment happened, I realized how deeply I loved you and only you."

"What happened?"

William shrugged. "Who can understand how the heart works? I just know that one day I loved you and the next I was madly in love with you. Remember the night we had three guys over?"

"Yeah, you fucked them until you were raw."

"I was trying to tell myself that everything was the same as it had been, that nothing had changed, but the entire evening I was picturing myself fucking you, making love to you."

"We've never slept together, Will."

"I know."

They were silent for a moment before Mike spoke again. "What happened, Will? How did we end up like this?"

William shrugged. "The heart changes and the love grows stronger. I'm sorry, I should have told you sooner rather than being a melodramatic queen."

"So what do we do now?"

"Let's go on a date. Just you and me and no third parties."

"Will, we can't date, we're married!"

"I'm just asking for a way to get to know you again. Please say yes?"

Mike didn't have to think about it. His own love for

William, held in check throughout the years, was growing stronger. "Is tonight good for you?"

Chapter Twenty One

Nancy's phone rang.

He looked at it and scowled. He answered it anyways. "What do you want, fucker?"

Devon chuckled. "I suppose I deserved that for how I treated you."

"Damn right. You're even lucky I'm picking up the Goddamned motherfucking phone!"

"I know I am. I'm lucky you still want to talk to me."

"Who says I want to?"

"You answered the phone, didn't you?"

"Look motherfucker, just start talking."

"I don't want to do this on the phone. Can I take you out to lunch today?"

Nancy huffed. "Fine, be here in five minutes."

"I can do better than that."

There was a knock at Nancy's front door. "Hold on a second, someone's at my door." Nancy dropped his phone on the hallway table and pulled the door open. There stood Devon, his beautiful dark brown hair all dishevelled and his eyes looking all gorgeous.

"Hey," he said.

Nancy crossed his arms and blocked the door. "If you think I'm going to invite you in for a cup of tea, you can forget it, mister."

"I know I have to earn your trust again, but there is an explanation. I swear it."

Nancy grabbed his coat and phone and closed the door behind him. Locking it, he asked "You taking me to lunch now?"

"If you're willing."

"Fine, but you're paying."

"I know, I was going to anyways."

"Fine."

Nancy walked to the elevator and pressed the button. Then he turned and faced Devon, arms crossed.

"You're never going to forgive me, are you?"

"I will after I say this."

"Fine, lets hear it."

"I don't wait for no man, ever. If you want to date me, that's fine. If you want to fuck me, that's fine and dandy. But don't you dare ever keep me waiting."

"Okay, but if you're so mad, why are you talking to me?"

"Because I like you for fuck's sake, you idiot!"

"Oh." Devon stood there, subtly grinning. "Okay. I like you, too."

The elevator door opened and Nancy stepped into it with Devon following behind him. They both watched the door close.

Devon moved with liquid grace and pulled Nancy to him.

Nancy let him, let Devon kiss him and even kissed him back. It was better than he thought it would be, more powerful than he had expected.

Within seconds of being kissed and kissing back, Nancy forgot about being angry.

Chapter Twenty Two

Blaine reminded himself to stay calm. Breathe in, breathe out. He thought of Lamaze breathing and wondered if he would have to help Poppy through her birth. Oh God.

"You okay, handsome? You're breathing really funny," Justin asked.

Blaine blushed. "I guess I'm more nervous than I thought."

"Nothing to be nervous about. I just want to kiss your face off."

"That's what I'm nervous about."

"I'll be gentle, unless you want me to be rough." Justin held out his left hand. "Grab hold, handsome."

Blaine took Justin's hand and was surprised by how right it felt in his. They walked down the street and stopped in front of Blaine's building. "How did you know where I lived?"

"Where you live? I live here, just moved in. I have a one bedroom apartment on the sixth floor."

"I have a two bedroom on the third."

"You live here?! How come I've never seen you?!"

"I work weird hours and mostly keep to myself."

"You get out with your friends, though, so you're not a complete shut-in."

"Yeah, they get worried if I spend too much time on my own."

"Smart friends. So, your place or mine?"

Blaine took a leap of faith. "Mine, if you'd like."

Justin's answering grin lit up Blaine's spirits. "I'd love that. We can go to my place on the next date."

"There will be another date?"

"Of course, handsome. You don't think I'd kiss just

anyone, do you?"

"Um." Blaine's cheeks flared red. "I don't know."

"Rest assured, I don't. Yes, I'd like to see you again. Whenever you can, actually. I want to get to know you, all of you."

Blaine's blush deepened. "Okay. Um, the elevator. Yes."

"I have you flustered. You're even more cute flustered than when you blush."

Blaine let out a short laugh and wondered if the flutter that flew through him was what he thought it was. "I bet you say that to all the boys."

"No, just you."

When the elevator door closed, Justin moved slowly towards him and wrapped his arms around Blaine. Blaine let him, and when Justin kissed him, slowly and softly, Blaine kissed him back, tasted Justin with his tongue, savouring him.

When he pulled apart from him, Justin was smiling. "That was lovely. I like it when you take charge."

Blaine grinned. "Turned you on, did it?"

Justin took hold of Blaine's hand and moved it down to his crotch. Justin was hard as a rock. "What do you think?"

"Um..." He was saved from making a reply when the elevator dinged and opened on the third floor. "I-I'm down here."

"Don't be nervous, Blaine. Though it is kind of cute. I just hope it's not me that makes you nervous."

"More the situation. I haven't done this in a while."

Blaine led the way down the hallway. He stopped in front of his apartment door and got out his keys. Opening his door, he led Justin inside and closed the door behind them.

Then Justin was kissing him, and Blaine forgot to be nervous. All that existed was Justin.

Chapter Twenty Three

Justin's kiss was heavenly.

Blaine had never felt anything like this, not even with David. His kisses had been punctual and then cold compared to Justin's, which stirred a fire deep in his belly. The fire radiated out though his body, and all Blaine wanted to do was get Justin naked.

Which is why he broke the kiss and stepped away from him.

"I'll, um, give you the tour."

"What's the hurry?" Justin said. "I rather liked where this was going." He pulled Blaine back against him and Blaine had to fight his urge to run.

"I'm sorry."

"Never be sorry with me unless you're being an asshole. Don't ever apologize when you've done nothing wrong." He kissed Blaine quickly. "Let's have that tour."

Blaine took Justin through his apartment, showing him the living room, kitchen, and bathroom. He hesitated only a moment before opening the door to the second bedroom that he used as a studio.

"Holy shit," Justin said, turning to look around. "Did you paint those?"

"Yeah. I use this room as my studio."

"These are incredible. I mean that, I really do."

"They're just portraits."

"Don't be modest. These are incredible. There's Nancy and Chuck, there's Poppy. There's a woman I don't know."

"That's my grandmother, Nan."

"They're beautiful. And there's...."

He stopped. Blaine knew what he had seen. He had seen his own portrait. "Justin, I'm sorry, I should have asked your permission, I should have-"

"It's beautiful. You're beautiful."

Then Justin was kissing him again, and Blaine let him and kissed him back. He tried to put all of his feelings into the kiss, tried to communicate how amazing Justin made him feel with every exploration he made with his tongue.

This time it was Justin who broke the kiss. He was breathing heavily and looked at Blaine with want in his eyes.

"God, I want you."

"I want you, too. So much that it's frightening."

"Love is always frightening."

"Love? I didn't say anything about love."

"Isn't that what we're working towards?"

"I haven't loved anyone for a long time."

"Then let yourself love again, Blaine. Don't let that jerkwad who treated you so badly tarnish what we've got going on here."

Blaine pulled away. "I think you should go."

"Blaine, I'm sorry for saying that, but I'm not him, I'm not who he is."

"Please go. Please."

"Okay, but I want to see you tonight."

"Why are you doing this? Why do you want to see me again?"

"Because maybe I'm falling for you. I don't *want* to see you again, I *need* to. Promise me you'll see me tonight? I'll pick you up at seven."

Despite the answer he wanted to give, Blaine nodded. "Okay."

"Okay," Justin said. "Good." When he kissed Blaine this

time, it was soft and fleeting and Blaine wanted more. "Where do you want me to pick you up?"

"Just come and get me at The Cabin."

"Emergency meeting?"

"Yeah, you could say that."

"God, I hope they're on my side. I'll let myself out and I'll see you at seven on the dot. Okay?"

"Okay."

Blaine watched him leave and heard the door close. He stood in his studio and looked at Justin's painting. He didn't get him right.

Justin was far better looking in person.

Chapter Twenty Four

Not even bothering to knock, Blaine walked into Nan's kitchen. She was already making a jug of pink lemonade. Blaine stopped short. "How'd you even know I was coming?"

"Oh, a grandmother always knows. It's a thing she sees with her heart."

Blaine blinked at her. "Seriously?"

"No, Blaine, honey. I saw you coming up the walk. It doesn't take that long to make a jug of juice. You looked like you need it. Tell Nan what's wrong, go on, spill. You look like you've got butterflies in your legs and frogs in your belly. As it's normally the other way around, that can only mean one thing."

Sitting, Blaine took the cup of pink lemonade she held out to him. "Nan, I'm not dying."

"I know you're not dear, you're in love."

"What are you talking about?" Blaine tried to keep the nervousness out of his voice and the blush out of his cheeks. He was unsuccessful on both counts.

"I know you, Blainey boy. I've only seen you like this once before. You've met someone. Oh, isn't this lovely?"

"You mean I was like this with David?"

"No, Honey. You were like this with that Edward fellow. You weren't in love with David. You liked him a whole lot, to be sure, but not love." Nan took Blaine's hands in both of her own. "It's so good to see you like this again. I never gave up hope."

Blaine hadn't thought of Edward in years. He had been Blaine's first serious relationship. It wasn't that they were merely boyfriends, there seemed to be a real connection between them. Edward had only been the third guy he had slept with, but it was more than that. He honestly and truly loved him.

"Thanks Nan, I needed to think about him today."

"Blaine, honey, the fact that you still feel pain over the loss of Edward is testament to how much you loved him. You were like this with Edward and you're like this now. So tell me." She poured her own glass of juice. "Who is the lucky man?"

"Nan, it's just been a couple of dates."

"Does he work at the library?"

"How would you know a thing like that?"

"Ms. Robinson told me at the hair salon this morning. She said you and he had quite the reaction to each other and then left the library together after your shift. So who is he? Does he have a big family? Does he have a big cock?"

Blaine spit out a mouthful of pink lemonade. "Jesus, Nan!"

"Well, I'm just concerned for you, honey. I know that Ms. Robinson wouldn't hire a crazy person and it's lovely that you've found each other; I just don't want you to get hurt."

"Nan, we haven't done that yet."

"Oh." She stood and got a cloth from the sink to mop up the juice on the tabletop. "That's good, dear."

"His name is Justin. He survived an emergency meeting of the guys at the Cabin."

"He was able to hold his own?" Nan turned back towards Blaine with her eyebrows raised. "That is impressive. What does Nancy think? I've always trusted his judgement. Mike is good too, of course, but Chuck always has his pecker out."

"Nan."

"Well, he does. Always looking for the next hole-in-one. Must have an incredible golf club. So, is Justin nice? Do you like him?"

"Yes, Nan."

"Then what's the problem?"

"He's also the father of the baby that Poppy is going to have."

Nan clutched her bosom in shock. "No! I thought Poppy was a lesbian!"

"She is."

"And what about Justin? Isn't he gay?"

"He is."

Nan sat back down at the table. She looked stunned. "Oh, Blaine, honey. I don't think pink lemonade is going to help you in this."

She was silent for a moment, before she took his hands in hers again. "Trust in yourself. Follow your heart. If you love Poppy, you can love someone she was with. Trust in yourself, Blaine. That's all I can say. Trust in yourself and follow your heart."

Blaine was touched by his grandmother's words but spoke the truth. "Nan, I'm afraid. What if I fuck this up? I really like him."

"It's okay to be afraid, Blaine, but you can't be afraid of what ifs. That's no way to live. Just take it moment by moment. Now, finish your lemonade and don't spit out any more or I'll be cleaning it up all afternoon."

Chapter Twenty Five

Chuck was nervous. He had never been nervous about meeting a guy before. Usually by now, he would have fucked the guy and moved on to the next one; the deed would be done and that was it. Yet, here he was, driving to Sebastian's place, and he was as nervous as if he were on his first date and about to have sex for the first time.

Sebastian drove, his eyes on the road but his hand on Chuck's left leg. It was warm, and Chuck wondered if the rest of him would be as hot to touch. When Sebastian reached further and his hand brushed Chuck's cock, Chuck was instantly hard.

Sebastian chuckled. "Someone's ready to go."

"Sorry, I'm a little pent up."

"Nothing to be sorry about. I like that I make you hard."

"You have no idea."

"Well, you've been a good boy. The least I can do is give you your reward."

"I have a feeling I'm going to like this reward."

"You'll have to wait and see," Sebastian said with a smile. He turned into a parking spot and turned off the car. "You'll also have to calm down. I don't want to scare any of the neighbours with the size of that thing." He flicked Chuck's cock and Chuck let out a small moan.

"You know I like the rough stuff."

Sebastian undid his seat belt. "You think you do, but you're just a big softie. You're looking for love just like the rest of us. The rough stuff thing is just a cover."

Chuck narrowed his eyes. "Really? You think so?"

"I know so. I haven't done anything but touch your leg and

you're as hard as a rock. That wouldn't have happened if you only got turned on by the rough stuff."

"It's all I know."

"So get to know something else. Get to know me."

"I thought that's what we were coming here to do."

"No, we were coming here to fuck each other. That has nothing to do with getting to know each other. What I've gotten to know about you, I really like. I want to know more about you, Charlie."

Chuck's breath caught in his throat. "I do too. Want to know more about you, I mean."

"So let's go do something fun instead of fucking. What's your favourite place in the city?"

"I thought fucking was fun."

"No, that's play time. Come on, tell me what your favourite place is."

Chuck was silent for a moment, not sure how to respond. Finally he decided on the truth. "The amusement park."

"Good choice. What's your favourite ride?"

Chuck sighed. "You're going to laugh at me."

"No I won't. I promise. What's your favourite ride?"

"The merry-go-round," Chuck said quietly.

Sebastian's eyes widened in surprise and he let out a bark of laughter.

Chuck crossed his arms. "See, I said that you were going to laugh at me."

"I'm sorry, I'm sorry, I just expected you to say a roller coaster or something. I didn't expect that!" Sebastian started the car again.

"Where are you going? I thought we were going to fuck?"

"Oh we will. But seeing you on a merry-go-round is too good to pass up!"

Chapter Twenty-Six

Poppy wondered if today was the day.

River Moon Falls, AKA Connie, was back in the kitchen. It must not have gone well at work again this morning, as she was once again holding a big knife. She was massacring some kind of meat. Poppy didn't want to eat whatever she was 'cooking'. It would probably give her indigestion.

She rubbed her belly protectively. "Wish me luck, little one," she whispered.

Poppy entered the kitchen just as Connie took a particularly hard swing with her knife and severed more of the meat. Poppy saw that it was actually a whole pig, and the latest swing had cut off one of its hind legs. Poppy tried hard not to gag and said, "There's no way I'm going to eat that."

"Oh, look who decided to come home! I've been out working all day! It must be nice to have a trust fund and be independently wealthy!"

Huffing out a breath, Poppy told herself to be calm. "You know I don't have a trust fund. It's my money, I made it from modelling."

"Well you can't do any of that anymore, you're getting fat."

Poppy had finally had it. "I'm not fat, Connie. I'm pregnant."

It was as if Poppy had set off a silent bomb in the room. Connie's face turned several shades of red and then progressed to a purple colour. When she finally spoke, her voice was a wheeze. "How did this happen?"

"You know, everyone keeps asking me that. If I have to tell you how a baby was made, then we've got big problems."

The purple of Connie's face turned to puce. "You whore!

You've gone back to men! Does what we have together mean nothing to you?"

"And what exactly do we have together, Connie?"

"My name is River Moon Falls!"

"Oh spare me the spiritual crap, okay? I fell in love with Connie, but I don't like River Moon very much."

"So you're going to leave me for a man? I thought you hated dick! You told me you did!"

"I did and still do. I went out and got drunk one night and one thing led to another. This shit happens, Connie."

"Oh, dykes sleeping with shit bag men happens all the time! How could I have been so blind? You've been fucking him this entire time behind my back!"

"Oh, Connie. It was a one-time thing, that's all it was. Just a bit of comfort."

"But I could have comforted you! It's my job!"

"You don't look too comforting when you're holding a meat cleaver. And it shouldn't be your job, you should want to. It's not a duty, it's a privilege."

There was silence in the kitchen for a moment, broken only by the drip of blood from the meat cleaver onto the floor. "So what happens now? Are you going to carry on fucking Mr. Happy?"

Poppy had finally had it. "No. I want you to move out." Once the words were out, it was as if a weight had lifted from her whole body.

Connie looked stricken. "You can't mean that. We've been together for five years!"

"Which is like thirty in lesbo years. I do mean it. I wanted to work things out, but this angry you just takes over everything. You've forgotten how to be happy. I wouldn't have gone looking for comfort if you were actually here instead of here in body but not in mind."

"So what happens now?"

"I want you out. Take your shit and leave. You have forty-eight hours. Then I want you gone. And for God's sake, get rid of the pig, won't you? You're bleeding all over my floor."

Chapter Twenty Seven

Nancy lay naked beside Devon and they shared a cigarette. The smoke furled up to the ceiling and looked like the afterthoughts of clouds. He should write that down, he thought.

Devon stubbed out the cigarette and lit two more, passing one to Nancy. He took a puff of his cigarette and let out a mouthful of smoke. Reaching over, he tweaked Nancy's left nipple. "Why so quiet, Clarence?"

Nancy slapped his hand away. "Don't call me that, you hot fuck."

Laughing, Devon leaned back against the headboard. "Okay, okay. But what's wrong? Was it not good for you?"

"It was very good. You've got a huge dick, you're an attentive lover, and you can fuck like a racehorse. That's a problem."

"Well it sounds good to me. Why is that a problem?"

"Because I started off mad at you. You'll fuck me but you won't talk to me."

"We're talking now."

"Well then maybe you can tell me why you stood me up."

Devon looked uncomfortable. "Nancy..."

"If you're going to give me some bullshit excuse, you can stop talking now. It's not because you were in the closet, because you work in a fucking gay bar. I don't know what's going on with you, but I can't stay away from you for some reason. I just can't. So we have to clear the air, or I'll never be able to trust you."

"Nancy..."

"Don't you 'Nancy' me, motherfucker. You were weird on

the phone before and you stood me up, and then you show up at my place and we have ball-busting sex. The sex was amazing, but I want to connect with you and I can't do that if we have secrets."

Devon butted out his cigarette and lit another one. The smoke was filling the air of Devon's bedroom, and it looked as if a storm was moving in to match Nancy's mood. "You won't like it when I tell you," Devon said.

"Honey, whatever you have to tell me, just fucking say it. What's the big mystery? Why did you get weird on me and then show up out of the blue? What's going on, Devon?"

Devon was silent for a long time. Nancy wasn't even sure that he would speak but when he did, Nancy wished he hadn't. He wished that they had stayed in their silent cocoon instead, just fucking their brains out. The words could not be taken back, could not be erased.

"I got scared."

"Well honey that's fine, everyone gets frightened."

"That's not it, Nancy. I don't make much working at The Cabin as a bartender, you know."

"Honey, I don't care about money. You have to know that."

"Please, let me finish. I was with a client that afternoon. It was very unexpected, but he was a high-paying client and I couldn't turn down the money, I just couldn't."

Nancy took a drag off his cigarette. "What kind of client was it?" he said slowly.

Devon stubbed out the cigarette and lit another. "He paid me three hundred dollars for three hours of my time."

"Devon, what are you saying?"

The smoke in the room was furious now and Nancy knew the storm was about to blow. He wanted Devon to stop speaking, to stop saying anything, but it was too late.

"I'm a male escort," Devon said. "Men pay to have sex with me."

Chapter Twenty Eight

The drive didn't take long. Before Chuck knew it, they'd arrived at the amusement park. "I still can't believe you want me to ride a merry-go-round. That's not a very sexy date." They got out of the car and started walking across the parking lot.

"Get your mind off fucking for a while," Sebastian said. "In the dating game, this is called getting to know one another."

"I already know that I want to know you."

"No, we both know that we want to fuck each other. I knew the moment I saw you in the bathhouse. I want to fuck you right now. But a big tough guy like you, riding on a plastic horse? Can't pass that up."

"This is torture."

"No, it's called a date. Or would you rather fuck me and be done with me?"

"No!" Chuck was surprised by how much he wanted to continue seeing Sebastian. It was actually more important to him at this point than fucking him. "No," he said again. "I want to get to know you, too."

Sebastian took Chuck's hand in his. "Good, let's go find your ride."

Chuck didn't need to look for it. He ran toward it, pulling Sebastian after him. Within moments, they stood in front of the merry-go-round, the horses looking strong and fierce, but somehow welcoming and fun at the same time.

Sebastian smiled watching him. "Which one's your favourite?"

"Oh, it doesn't matter, they're all the same."

"No, they're not. Everyone has a favourite horse. Which

one's yours?"

"You're going to laugh."

"No I won't, I promise."

Blushing, Chuck said "The pink one."

There was a second where Sebastian was able to hold back the laughter, but it finally broke out and soon they were both laughing, holding on to each other to keep from falling over.

Wiping at the tears in his eyes, Sebastian kissed Chuck full on the lips. "Okay tough guy, let's go get you your pink horse."

"There's a kid on it, he's still riding."

"Not for long."

Chuck watched as Sebastian got up on the ride and went over to the kid. Taking out his wallet, he took out a twenty dollar bill and gave it to the kid, whispering to him. The kid nodded and got off right away, rushing into the crowd, his money clutched in his fist.

"Okay cowboy, saddle up."

Chuck swung himself up onto the horse and was surprised when Sebastian got on the pink horse behind him. "You don't have to ride with me."

"I want to. We can be close this way."

The ride, normally a little boring, was made all the more exciting with Sebastian pressed so close to him. Chuck had never felt this way with any guy, with anyone. Every time he felt Sebastian's breath on the back of his neck, it sent shivers down his spine and his nipples hardened. His heart was racing and he was dizzy every time Sebastian touched him.

As the ride ended and the merry-go-round stopped turning, Chuck was finally able to put a word to what he was feeling.

He was in love with Sebastian.

Chapter Twenty Nine

Blaine noticed the change in all of them. They were different. The differences were subtle, but they were there. Mike's eyes had taken on a faraway look. Nancy was tense and on edge; even his laughter was different. Chuck looked lost and somewhat afraid, but happy at the same time.

"I need a mickey of vodka," Chuck said.

Nancy took one look at him and smiled. "Someone got bitten by the love bug."

"Shut up, I did not."

"I know that love look, and I'm never wrong."

"Can I just get a fucking drink?"

"Let the boy breathe," Mike said. "He hasn't even had a chance to sit down yet."

"Let's all get a round," Blaine said. "My treat."

"As per usual," Mike said.

"Yes, heaven forbid any of you actually pay for your own booze," Blaine said. He motioned for the waiter and Devon walked over to their table.

Nancy stiffened immediately. "Hello," he said to Devon. His voice was oddly polite and formal. Devon looked at Nancy and smiled slightly.

"Hello, Nancy."

He took their order and left. Blaine turned to Nancy. "What's up with you?"

Nancy looked down for a minute. "Nothing."

"Yes, there is. You never get all weird around a guy. You were practically formal with him." Blaine said. "You're always goading me into telling you what's wrong with me. So spill."

Nancy looked up and Blaine was startled. Nancy had

never looked this way, so frightened and unsure of himself. "I think I love him."

"Devon?"

"Yes, fucking Devon."

"So what's wrong? You've always believed in love."

"He told me he's a fucking prostitute."

"So he sleeps with women?" Chuck said. "That's kind of gross."

"No, dipshit. He sleeps with men."

"Oh," Chuck said. He was quiet for a beat and then said, "That's actually kind of hot."

"Don't do it, don't get involved with him," Mike said. "You'll end up losing him to another man."

"Says the man who's going on a date with his husband," Nancy said.

"Testify," Blaine said and clinked his bottle against Nancy's martini glass.

"Mmm-hmmm. When's that happening anyways?" Nancy asked.

"Tonight. I'm so nervous. I mean, what if I screw everything up?"

"You're married to him." Nancy pointed out. "That's gotta be some kind of safety net, right?"

"We've never slept together!" Mike said. "What do I do? What if he wants to have sex? We've never had sex!"

"Do you love him?" Nancy asked.

"God yes."

"Do you find him attractive?"

"Absolutely."

"Then go with the flow and get to know him again."

"Then you have to get to know Devon." Blaine said. "Tell him you're uncomfortable with the whole prostitute thing, but you have to see him. If you think you love him, you have to give him a chance."

Nancy, Chuck, and Mike all looked at him open-mouthed. Nancy snapped his fingers and took a sip of his drink. "Nice to have you back, Blaine. What's going on with you and Justin?"

"I'm in love with him. I'm terrified and I'm scared that I'll get hurt. But I'm going to tell him. I want it to grow into something. I don't know if it's too soon, but I don't care."

"Oh honey, you have no idea how good that sounds. What made you change your mind? What was the click?"

"I showed him his portrait. He didn't freak out, told me that he was falling for me, and I realized I was falling for him, that I had already fallen."

"God, when did we all start loving somebody? What the fuck happened?" Chuck said.

"What? You're not in love," Blaine said.

"I am. With Sebastian."

"That guy you met at the bathhouse? How's he in the sack?"

"I wouldn't know. We haven't slept together yet."

There was silence again. Now everyone was looking at Chuck, open-mouthed with shock. "What do you mean? You've been seeing him for almost a week now." Nancy asked, "You haven't slept together yet?"

"Nope," Chuck said. "Not once."

"Holy shit," Mike said.

"Mary and Joseph's Technicolor dream coat," Nancy said.

"Fuck really? Not once?" Blaine asked.

"Nope," Chuck said, "and I'm in love with him."

Just then, Justin walked through the front doors of The Cabin. When he saw Blaine, he smiled and began to walk towards them.

Nancy saw him approaching and clapped his hands together. "Meeting adjourned for now, ladies. We have company."

Chapter Thirty

Nancy stood and hugged Justin. "Thank you."

Justin hugged him back and grinned. "You're welcome. But I didn't do anything, yet."

"Oh yes you did. Now you two go on, get, go out into the night. I've got a barkeep I have to talk to. And you," he turned to Mike. "Stop being a douchebag and go home and fuck your man." He turned to Chuck. "And you, call him up and spend time with him. I'm taking my leave, it's been fun."

Nancy picked up his martini glass and downed the last mouthful and sashayed off to the bar. They all watched him go.

"Well, smell her!" Chuck said. "She's a woman on a mission."

"We all have our missions," Blaine said. "We have to go out and see them through, no matter how afraid we are."

Justin looked at him, his eyes wide, a smile playing on his mouth. "Blaine?"

"I'm not afraid anymore," Blaine said.

When Justin moved in to kiss him, Blaine wrapped his arms around him and pulled him close and kissed him first. He tried to put everything he had not been able to communicate, or had been too afraid to, into the kiss. Mike and Chuck and the rest of the bar ceased to exist. All that filled him was the touch of Justin's lips on his and the sound of their heartbeats beating as one.

"God, get a room," Mike said. "You're going to be fucking and sucking in a moment and, while I'm happy for you, Blaine, I just don't want to see that."

Blaine pulled away from the kiss, the heat from Justin's

lips still keeping him warm. "Sorry guys."

"Don't be sorry!" Chuck said. He rose and slapped each of them on the back. "I'm going to go get me some! And you should too, Mike, stop being a douchebag."

"Fuck you," Mike said. "I don't need this abuse, I have a man who loves me at home."

"So then fuck him. Later gents!" Chuck tapped a finger to his hat in salute and left. Mike got up to leave but stayed for a moment, looking at Justin.

"I guess it falls to me to say this but if you hurt him, we'll find you and hurt you."

"Mike!" Blaine said.

"It's okay, Blaine." Justin held out a hand to Chuck. "I wouldn't have it any other way. I want to honour him and love him. That's all."

"Good. You're much better-looking than David. I'm glad to see that Blaine's taste in men is improving." He gave them both a grin and took his leave.

Standing next to Justin, Blaine could feel a pulse emanating from him. Blaine didn't know if it was because his dick was hard or because he wanted Justin so much, but didn't care. He just wanted him.

"Should we stay and have a drink?" Justin asked. "I could use a bit of liquid courage."

"Why? You're not afraid, are you?"

"Terrified. I haven't been this nervous to be with a guy in a long time."

Blaine blushed. "You do a good job of hiding it. Why are you nervous?"

"Because you're you. You're funny, intelligent, kind-hearted. You can stop me any time, you know."

"Oh no, keep going. What else am I?"

Justin laughed. "You're incredible."

"You make me feel incredible."

Justin shook his head. "No, you always were. You're just beginning to realize it now."

"My Nan would love you."

"Good, so that's a future date."

"To meet my Nan?"

"Yes, but right now I want to finish my drink and take you home."

"No, we'll go to mine."

Chapter Thirty One

Blaine was oddly calm. He knew that he shouldn't be, that he should have a rioting mess of worms filling his stomach. He should be sweating, stammering, shaking inside of himself.

He wasn't. Blaine didn't know what this meant, what this change in him was. He had been afraid for months, terrified of stepping out into the world. He had the people he talked to on the phone, but that had been it as far as dates were concerned for months now.

It was as if he were crawling out of a dark hole of his own making. He painted this afternoon to work on his pent up energy. He was going to show the painting to Justin tonight. He was going to try to explain what he had achieved.

Justin took his hand when they entered the elevator. Justin's skin was warm to the touch, and Blaine held on to it, taking comfort from his grasp instead of fearing it. Justin squeezed his hand.

"You okay? You're oddly quiet tonight."

"I'm better than okay."

"You sure? You're normally stammering by now. I try to distract you by kissing you. Tonight doesn't seem to be that kind of evening."

"Oh, it will be."

"It will?" Justin grinned.

"I want to show you. It'll make more sense when I show you."

"Oh God, you're not a naked acrobat are you? Because that would be totally hot, especially if you wore something in tight spandex."

Blaine let the laughter erupt out of him. It was such a

strange sound coming from his mouth, so unfamiliar. Leaning forward, he kissed Justin, putting all of his heart into it, not holding anything back.

Justin welcomed him by wrapping his arms around him, pressing himself against him. Blaine held on to him and let his fingers run through Justin's hair. They only pulled apart when someone cleared their throat behind them.

Blaine turned and realized the elevator doors had opened and Poppy was standing there with a large smile on her face. "Hey boys!" She held up a bottle of apple cider and held it out to Blaine. "Here, honey."

"What's this?" Blaine was confused. He stepped out of the elevator and Justin followed him, taking hold of his hand.

"Well, I was coming by to see if you wanted company, but it seems like you already have some. Hey, Justin."

"Hey, Poppy."

"Why Justin, are you blushing? Blaine usually does that!"

"No, no, it must be the light."

"Poppy, did you need something? Is everything okay?"

"I'm fine, I'll tell you tomorrow. You've got plans tonight from the looks of it. I may be a fag hag, but I'm also a lesbian and I know when it looks like someone's going to get some."

She leaned in and kissed Justin briefly on the cheek. "Thank you."

"Why does everyone keep thanking me?"

"Oh, honey, you have no idea." Poppy wiggled her fingers at them. "Have fun, boys."

They watched her go. Justin turned to Blaine. "What is all this about?"

"I'll tell you. But first, I want to show you something."

Unlocking the apartment door, he went in and turned on the light. What he wanted to show Justin was standing in the living room, waiting for them. Justin had stopped in the middle of the room, transfixed by the canvas on display.

Chapter Thirty Two

It was bigger than his normal paintings, and it wasn't a portrait. Instead it was an expression of everything he had held inside of him for so long. It was an expression of emotion, of the anger he had experienced, the hurt he had endured.

"I didn't think a portrait would be enough." Blaine said. He walked towards Justin and put his hand out. Justin took it and Blaine took strength from his touch.

"It's incredible. It moves me, but what is it?"

"That's what I want to tell you."

Justin turned to him, taking him in his arms. "What is it? You know you can tell me anything, right? I'm not going to run away."

"There's a reason I've hidden for so long, why I'm so afraid of you. It all has to do with David, with who I let him turn me into. Everyone could see that David was controlling, cold. Nancy even said he was cruel. They didn't know the half of it. They had no idea, not Nancy, Mike, or Chuck. My Nan knew, but she wouldn't probe me about it. She knew I would talk in my own good time."

"Talk about what, Blaine?"

His brown eyes were filled only with concern, with empathy. They were not the cold blue seas that he had endured. Blaine took a deep breath and closed his eyes. When he opened them again, he was okay. Justin was still there, still holding him, and he was all right.

"David hit me. At first, it was a casual slap or nudge on the body with his fist. Then he started punching me. Never where anyone could see, never where it would show."

"Why didn't you leave?" Justin's voice was a whisper. "You

could have gotten help, Blaine."

"I was too afraid to. Too petrified. He had worn me down to nothing. He told me I was garbage. He made me feel like I *was* nothing. He yelled at me all the time, told me I was worthless, that I was shit. The thing is, I believed him. That's the part that I regret."

"Blaine..." Justin's fingers tightened on his arms, and he pulled him closer. Then Justin wrapped his arms around him as if to protect him. Blaine took strength from his closeness, from the scent of him.

"Blaine, you're not nothing. You have no idea how special you are."

"Thank you for saying that. The thing is, I'm afraid. I got away from David, but I still miss him. I used to think about him every day. He's been in my mind every day for five months."

"What do you think of now?"

"You," Blaine said. "All I can think of at night is you. You've been in and out of my dreams, I think about you at work, when I'm with the guys, when I'm with my Nan."

"I think about you, too. I can't get you out of my mind."

"Justin, there's something else I want to tell you."

Justin put a finger to Blaine's lips and then kissed him. "It's okay, Blaine. You don't have to say it yet. I know exactly how feel. I feel the same way. We have time yet, there's no need to rush. I'm with you for the long haul."

"I was hoping you'd say that."

"So, the canvas. That was you letting go of what he put you through?"

"Yes. I'm letting it go and setting myself free. I'm not going to be afraid that another man will treat me that way. I refuse to live in fear."

"You're one strong, incredible man, Blaine."

"I know," he said simply.

"So, what happens now?"

"This," Blaine said, and kissed him.

Chapter Thirty Three

Poppy knocked on Nan's door.

It was still light out. The air was warm with the scent of lilacs. She wondered if she was communicating every moment to her child through her eyes, if her unborn child could see what she was seeing.

Holy fuck, she thought. I'm starting to sound like Connie. That's really not good. I have to have a drink or a cigarette or something.

The door opened and   Nan enveloped Poppy in a big hug. "Come in, dear, I made you pink lemonade. I put a bit of water in, so it's not so acidic. The way Blaine likes it will pucker even your asshole. Come in, come in!" Poppy did so and she closed the door behind her.

Nan's house had always been a home away from home. Poppy had known Nan for as long as she'd known Blaine, about ten years. Never having grown up with a grandmother, Poppy cherished her.

Nan went into the kitchen and put a glass of juice on the table and took a seat, her own mug of tea in front of her. "Blaine tells me there are some congratulations in order."

"I told Blaine not to tell you, I wanted to tell you myself!"

"Oh, honey, did you really think he wouldn't tell me, when he's in love with this Justin fellow?"

"You think they're in love already?" Poppy took a sip of juice and continued. "That's pretty fast, even for fags."

"You are either afraid of the immediate connection or you embrace it. It does happen, you know."

"What are you talking about? Not true love?"

"Yes, dear, I am. It exists and it happens. Haven't you had

a really wild night with a woman, where you experienced a real connection, even for that night? Even if it's only for an evening, a day, a week, you love her."

Giving her a look of confusion, Poppy put down her glass. "Nan, I think you should stay away from the sherry."

"I drink gin, thank you very much, but I have to ask you, what do you think of this Justin fellow? Is he a good man? Will he treat him well?"

"You mean will he get pushed around again like he did with David? No, Justin is not like that."

"You know this, yet you only spent a night with him." Nan nodded her head as if agreeing with herself. "You see? True love does exist, even between someone like you and Justin. You're making a life. You chose to keep it and so Justin will be a part of your life forever."

"Nan, it's okay, Justin really is a wonderful man. He's one of the good ones." Poppy took her hands in hers. "It'll be okay, Nan."

"I just don't want to see him hurt again. He's such a sensitive boy, hiding all the time. I don't want him to hide again."

"He won't, Justin and I will make sure of it."

"Good. Now, onto another matter, what did Ms. River Moon Falls think of the whole baby thing? I presume you told her?"

"Yeah, I kicked her out. I had too much of her holier than thou attitude."

"Good for you dear! I never could stand the bitch!" Nan got up and got a bottle of vodka from her cupboard. "Here dear, have a little drop. You earned it." She poured a generous drop into Poppy's glass.

"I can't drink when preggers, Nan."

"Oh now, I don't know. I had a drop every now and again with Blaine's mother and she turned out fine." She paused. "Well, she turned out to be a bitch, but that's her own doing, not mine."

She clinked her glass against Poppy's "Drink up dear! To good things. For you and for Blaine."

"I'll drink to that, and finding a new woman."

"Oh, you will, dear, but we'll add that to the list." She clinked her tea mug against Poppy's glass twice more. "Now, are there any lesbian bars in the city?"

"Yeah, the Delphic Oracle."

"Oh, good name. So, why not go out and do a bit of muff diving?"

Poppy spit out her juice. Nan sighed and handed her a wet cloth.

"Today's youth are shocked far too easily," she said.

Chapter Thirty Four

Mike got home and rushed through the door. "Will, it's me, I'm sorry I'm late, I..." He noticed the state of the apartment.

There were candles everywhere, flickering from every surface. The table had been laid out with their best plates and glimmered as if there were jewels covering the wood. Standing there was William, dressed to the nines and holding a single rose. "Table for two, sir?" William grinned at Mike and held out his hand with a flourish. "Right this way."

"What is all this?" Mike wondered for a moment if he had stepped into the wrong apartment. "What's going on?"

"Well, you wanted to go on a date, right?" William said. "So there's no reason we can't have one right here."

"I, um, thought we were going out?"

"Why?" William picked up a bottle of red wine and poured a glass for both of them. "Are you nervous?"

Mike let out a breath. "God, yes."

"There's no reason to be. We loved each other enough to get married. Just relax. Dinner will be ready in about ten minutes."

Mike let out a nervous laugh. "Why are you doing all this?"

"All of what?"

"This!" Mike waved his hand around the room and at William. "You've never been this romantic before! Never once, in five years."

"You haven't seen anything yet." William leaned forward and took Mike's lips in a kiss. He tasted of wine and something more. "That I promise you."

"Why didn't you tell me you loved me?"

"Why didn't you?"

"God, I don't know!" Mike pushed his chair back and stood, walking away from the table. "This is all too much, just too much"

William stood and moved towards Mike. "We love each other, why is this too much?"

"Because I've loved you from the first moment I laid eyes on you. I've dreamed of having you and only you forever, for a long as I can remember." Mike was almost crying now, but he didn't care. "I have to get this out, have to get past this, or we can't go any further."

William looked at him, a quizzical look on his face. Then it softened, and William smiled. "All right, you drama queen, come here." He sat on the couch and patted the seat beside him.

Mike was terrified, but he went to his husband, suddenly unsure of how to be around him. When William reached out to take one of his hands in his, Mike almost pulled away. William must have sensed this and held on more tightly to his hand.

"Do you know when I first fell in love with you?"

"When?"

"It was three years ago. You made us dress up for Halloween. Do you remember?

"Yeah, I dressed up as Frank-N-Furter and you dressed up as Riff Raff from *The Rocky Horror Picture Show*."

"Exactly. You came out of your shell that day. You did it for me, because I know you don't love the movie as much as I do."

Mike smiled. "It has its moments."

William nodded and continued. "I thought to myself that anyone who would put on fishnets and makeup for me... well, it got to me. You got to me. I had loved you the entire time, but I finally saw it that night."

"Why did you take so long to tell me? I thought all you wanted was to screw around with other people. I mean, we've never even had sex!"

"I don't know. I don't know why it took so long, but I'm telling you now. I don't want to lose this, or you."

When William leaned in to kiss him, Mike let him. He tried to communicate all his love for William into that one kiss. Soon, they were breathing hard and Mike started pulling at William's shirt so he could feel him, touch all of him.

William broke the kiss and looked at him, lust in his eyes. "How hungry are you?"

"I'm hungry for you."

"Will you let me take you to bed?"

"Will dinner keep?"

"Who the fuck cares? Pizza goes good with red wine. We'll order in when we take our breather."

"Breather? Before what?"

"Before we do it all over again. I've waited this long to fuck you, the first time will probably go quick." William grinned. "It's always better the second time, wouldn't you agree?"

Mike warmed inside and he let the last of his wall down, let the worry go. Will stood and held out his hand. "Lead the way."

Chapter Thirty Five

Nancy waited for him.

The night had started out well. He had approached Devon, the love he held within him making him swagger. Nancy wasn't sure when the switch had turned, but he was beyond smitten. If Devon agreed to give up hooking, Nancy was all his. It was as simple as that.

He sashayed into the bar, looking for Devon, and saw him at the bar. He was serving a man a glass of beer. He was a tall gentleman with bright blond hair, a tan, and scruff covering his chin. He leaned in and spoke to Devon, and Devon nodded. The man with the blond hair got up and went to the washroom.

Devon followed him in moments later, leaving the bar unmanned.

Nancy waited for him, counting the seconds, his heart breaking a little each time. The shards of it filling his body. They flowed through his blood like ice freezing from the inside out. Five minutes later, the blond came out first, followed right behind by Devon. Nancy saw the blond give Devon twenty bucks and take off back into the crowd.

Devon started back to the bar. That's when he saw Nancy. He stopped for a moment, as if Nancy had hit him. Devon continued walking, taking up his station behind the bar. "Hey," he said.

"Hey yourself, cocksucker." Nancy surprised himself with how cold his voice sounded, but it didn't matter. None of it mattered now.

"Nancy..."

"Don't you motherfucking 'Nancy' me. We were together

last night and you're already sucking another guy's cock this evening?"

"He was my third client for today." His voice was soft. Not as if he was ashamed of what he had done or as if he were pleading. He was trying to calm Nancy down.

Nancy, for one, was not in a mood to be calm. "Your third client?"

"Nancy, it's what I do for a living, how I stay alive."

"Well, can't you do anything else? Like get a regular job for fuck's sake? Shit, I like sex and fucking as much as any other gay man, but why would you have sex that doesn't mean anything?"

"I get paid so I can support myself. Surely you understand that."

"No, I don't understand. I don't. I came here to tell you that I was in love with you. That if you stopped the hooking, I would be yours free and clear. Obviously didn't mean that much to you."

"Nancy, don't be like that, we've only been talking for a week."

"I've been coming here for years!" Nancy screamed. He knew it was unladylike to scream at someone in a public place, but he didn't care. His emotions were getting the better of him. "You're telling me you never checked me out? Never once wondered who that ebony-skinned beauty was, a Queen amongst queens? Were you just hoping that I'd be another one of your clients?"

"That's not fair. You know I care about you."

"Oh, you care about me. That's so big of you. Bigger than your fucking cock or your heart, then."

Nancy knew he had overstepped himself when he saw the look on Devon's face. He turned away from Devon and almost ran towards the door. He heard Devon calling him but didn't turn around, just kept walking.

Hearing footsteps behind him, he turned just as Devon crushed his lips to Nancy's. Nancy let Devon kiss him, one last time.

Devon pulled away. "Nancy, please. You know how I feel about you. You know it here." He touched Nancy on the chest.

Nancy shook his head. "I can't, Devon. Seeing you go into that washroom, knowing what you did. I'm a one-man guy and I don't share my man with anyone."

"You can't ask me to change who I am."

"I'm not. I'm asking you to change what you do."

Nancy put his hand against Devon's cheek, just for a moment. Then he took it away, turned his back, and headed home.

Chapter Thirty Six

Sebastian answered on the first ring. "Hey, handsome. What're you up to? Are you done with the boys so quickly?"

"I'm standing outside of your building, actually."

"What? What do you mean?"

"I need to talk to you. Can you buzz me up?"

"I'll come down to let you in." The phone went silent.

Chuck began to pace back and forth, his nerves jangling and jingling. He had never been so pent up: with lust, with longing, with anxiety about whether or not he was even doing the right thing.

When the front door opened, he saw Sebastian. He was bathed in the light from the foyer behind him for a moment, as if he were some sort of angel. Then the front door closed. Sebastian walked towards him carrying a bottle of wine and two wine glasses in his hand.

"What are those for?"

"You sounded like you needed a drink."

Sebastian's dark hair was mussed and all Chuck wanted to do was run his hands through it. "I've already had a few, I'm okay."

"You, turning down a drink? What's got you so agitated?"

Chuck didn't mean to blurt it out, but the words just tumbled out of him. "I think I love you."

"Oh, you think you do?" Sebastian said. He went over to a car and put down the wine glasses. He took a corkscrew from his back pocket and started taking the cork out of the bottle.

"I mean, I know I do, but I don't know what I'm doing. I've never been in love before, I have no idea what I'm doing here, how to say this properly."

Sebastian got the cork free and poured out two generous glasses of wine. Handing one to Chuck, he smiled. "Cheers."

"Cheers to what?" Chuck's heart was racing. He took a large gulp of wine, and then another. "This is crazy, this is fucking nuts. I can't love you already, I can't. I'm not even sure how to love a guy, all I do is fuck and then move on, I'm a cowboy that way." He took another large mouthful, finishing the glass.

"Yes, you were quite the cowboy this afternoon when you were riding a pink horse," Sebastian said with a chuckle, finishing off his own wine and taking the glass back from Chuck. He turned to put them back on the hood of the car.

"Look at me, for fuck's sake, I'm being fucking serious here! I don't know what I'm doing, I'm afraid! I fucking love you!"

When Sebastian turned, there was only hunger in his eyes. Chuck welcomed him, kissing lips that tasted like wine and smoke. Sebastian's touch set Chuck's skin on fire, and he yearned to touch more of him, to touch all of him.

Sebastian stepped gently away. "We should take this upstairs. Unless you want to put on a show for the neighbours?" He kissed Chuck quickly, his lips soft and warm.

"But what happens now? I mean, with us?"

"Now? I'm going to take you upstairs, get you naked, and we'll fuck like rabbits."

Chuck's heart leapt into his throat and he was instantly hard. "But how do you feel about me? What are we going to do? I'm freaking out here."

"Charles." The use of his full name quieted him almost instantly. "I've been in love with you since we had dinner together after the bathhouse. That love grew when I saw you riding on the pink horse. Don't worry about tomorrow, just focus on today. Just focus on now."

When Sebastian leaned in to kiss him, Chuck let him and kissed him back for all it was worth. When Sebastian turned to lead the way to his apartment, Chuck wondered if he was heading toward sanctuary or stepping off a cliff.

Thirty-Seven

Blaine pressed the accept call button and another call came through. "Thank you for calling. How may I help you today?"

"Yes, I'm having a problem browsing the web."

"What seems to be the problem, Ma'am?"

"Well, I keep trying to move my mouse to where I want it to go, but can't get a good grip on it with my socks on."

Blaine shook his head. "I'm sorry, Ma'am? Did you say your socks?"

"Yes, but with my bare feet, it works much better. Is there a different kind of mousy I can use for sock feet?"

"Ma'am, where do you have the mouse?"

"Why on the floor, of course. The guy at the store said it was called a mouse, but it works like a pedal, doesn't it? I have a lovely antique Singer machine. I thought it worked like that."

"No, Ma'am. It goes on the table."

He walked her through the process of using the mouse with her hand and using her fingers to click the buttons. She laughed when she closed an Internet window.

"Oh, that's much faster! On the table, who would have thought."

"I'm glad it works, Ma'am."

"You mean that I work! This wasn't an Internet thingy at all, was it? You were very kind to help me."

"It's my pleasure, Ma'am."

"Oh, it's Moira Seagrave, but you can call me Mo. Thank you so much. I know that you'll make someone a wonderful and thoughtful husband."

"Yes, Ma'am, I hope to someday."

"Oh, I've offended you, haven't I?"

"Why do you say that?" Blaine was a little ruffled but he didn't think he had let it into his voice.

"I told you to call me Mo, and you're Ma'am-ing me again. Do you like men? You're one of those homo-sapiens?"

"Mo..."

"Oh, it's all right, dear. My brother has his Pedro, has for years now. I even walked with him in the Prideful parade last year. Do you have someone who knows how special you are?"

Blaine smiled and heat bloomed in his chest. "Yes, Mo, I do."

"Do you love him?"

"Yes, I do." He was surprised he could say it so easily, that the words came so readily to his lips to a stranger.

"Well, you tell him I said to take care of you."

"I will, Mo."

He logged off his computer and got his coat, almost running out of the building to head towards the GLBTQ library and towards Justin. When he exited his building, his heart almost stopped.

Waiting for him was David.

Chapter Thirty-Eight

Stunned motionless, all Blaine could do was look at David.

His blond hair was still long and pristine. His blue eyes just as cold and unfeeling as they used to be, as they always were. The sight of him after all this time stopped Blaine in his tracks—not out of love or desire, but out of fear.

This surprised him. Blaine had pined for what he had with David, had ached as if he had died instead of just having left him. He had lain for a week in his apartment with the lights off. A part of him had been ripped out when David left him. Now Blaine understood which part that was.

"What the fuck are you doing here?"

"I came for you, of course. Do you think I'd be standing outside this shitty building for nothing? Do you think I'm that stupid?"

"Come for me?" Blaine had to choke the words out of his mouth. He couldn't stop his voice from cracking on the words, raising in pitch and taking all of his breath.

"I'm ready to forgive you now." David walked towards him, approaching him with smooth stride's that spoke of confidence. "You've learned your lesson."

Blaine hated himself for shaking a little at his closeness. He remembered how he had just grown used to this, how he had accepted every punch and slap, every insult. How he had taken every slight, every jealous mood swing. Blaine had just accepted this was what he was worth.

However, that was then, and this was now. Justin had shown him what love really was. He wouldn't give that up for anything in the world. Not for anything or anyone.

"What lesson is that, you're a piece of shit? Yeah, it took

me a long time to learn, but it finally sunk in."

David's look of anger was instantaneous. "What did you say to me?"

"You heard me, you useless fuck. Or are you deaf, too?"

Lashing out, David grabbed hold of Blaine's wrist. "You better watch what you're saying to me."

"I spent years watching what I said to you!" He pulled his wrist away from David with such force that David stumbled. "I won't do that again."

Blaine turned away from David and began walking. With every step, the fear left him. With every step, he was making a choice between what he had left behind and what was waiting for him.

When the GLBTQ Library came into view, he quickened his pace. He almost ran through the doors and spotted Justin the moment he entered. He ran to him, bypassing patrons and several carts filled with books.

Justin saw him. "Blaine, hey, what's-"

That was all he was able to get out before Blaine's mouth was upon his. He tried to communicate what had happened, what choice he had made. He broke the kiss softly. "Thank you."

"You're welcome?" Justin said, dazed.

"I love you. So much."

"I love you too, Blaine."

There was the sound of clapping behind them. Blaine turned to see all of the patrons watching them and clapping, every single one of them with a smile on their face. One man stepped forward and said, "Must have borrowed a really good book!" and laughed at his own joke.

Over the laughter, Justin whispered: "What was that about? Not that I mind you kissing me, but there was an intensity in that kiss that wasn't there before."

"It doesn't matter," Blaine said and kissed him again.

Chapter Thirty-Nine

Nancy knocked and let himself into Nan's house. "Hello, sweet lady? Anyone home?"

Nan came out of the kitchen. "Clarence, sweetheart! You're early! I wasn't expecting you for another twenty minutes!"

"Yeah well, I ended my shift early. You can do that when you're the boss."

"Oh, how lovely! I made you a glass of pink lemonade. I put a shot of vodka inside of it. You sounded like you needed it over the phone." She hugged him, drawing him into her embrace as only Nan could. Her hugs always reminded him of his mother's.

Nan pulled away from him. "Now, what's got you upset, Clarence? You're not shining."

Nan was the only one who called him by his real name. She was the only one he allowed. She had tried to call him Nancy, but had trouble with it. She read his face now and smiled. "I just look at you and don't see a girl. I see you, Clarence. No sense calling you something else."

"I know, that's what you always say."

"Well, it's true. I remember when you used to try on my shoes with Blaine. You always looked fetching in my leopard print high heels."

Nancy smiled. "I loved those shoes."

"I know you did, Clarence. Why do you want to run away from who you were?"

"Well, because it's who I am that's important."

"I couldn't agree more. Now will you tell me what's wrong with you? Or do I have to spike your lemonade even more? I put in three shots."

"I feel like I could drink a whole bottle of vodka."

Nan put her hand on Nancy's. "It's that bad? Oh honey, spill."

"It's this guy I met…"

"You met a man, too? First Blaine falls in love, now you? Oh, this is wonderful! I wonder if it's something in the lemonade." Nan took a sip of her own drink. "No, still tastes the same. So who is he? Where did you meet him? Tell me everything."

"There's nothing to tell."

"Oh, yes there is. You're in love with him."

"I haven't told you anything yet, how could you possibly know that?"

"I'm not blind, Clarence. I know love when I see it. It's all over you. Blaine gets all worried when he's in love. You? You get all blustery and upset and stressed out. I've seen you in true love only once before." Nan took Nancy's hands in her own. "You get this look in your eyes that's wide as a pit you've fallen into. You only got that with that Lewis fellow."

Nancy tried to pull his hands away but Nan held firm. "I don't want to talk about that."

"Well, then just listen to what I have to say. Love is love, where ever you find it. You loved Lewis, but he wasn't ready for love. He did love you, but he wasn't ready for you. Clarence, you can't spend the rest of your life looking for love and running away from it when it finds you. What's so wrong with this new fellow?"

"Devon."

"What's so wrong with this Devon fellow?"

Nancy took a deep breath before speaking. "He's a male prostitute. I told him if he stopped it, I would be his, but he couldn't do that."

Nan took a moment of her own before speaking. "You can't change who a person is, Clarence. They do what they have to do. Besides, you already love him. I can hear it in your voice. You're running away from him. It has to be his choice to stop what he does, not yours." She patted his hand gently. "Besides, he's a male hooker for Christ's sake! Think of the positions he could do in the sack!"

Nancy spit out a mouthful of pink lemonade with a loud splutter. Nan shook her head and handed Nancy a cloth with a sigh and a smile upon her face.

Chapter Forty

Blaine looked up when a shadow fell over the check-out counter. His breath caught in his throat. It was David.

"I'd like to check this book out please."

"How did you find me?"

"Wasn't that hard, to be honest. Just had to wait for you to walk away for a little while, so intent on getting to your new man. He's quite the looker. Maybe I'll have him when I'm done with you."

"I already told you!" Blaine tried to keep his voice quiet, but the emotions came to the surface, boiling like lava. His blood ran hot at the fact that David would come here, that David had followed him. There was no way to hold the feelings back now that he had found a way to let them free. "Leave me the fuck alone! I don't belong to you and never did. I'm sorry it took me so long to realize what a shit you are!"

He was screaming now, tears running down his face. Oddly, Blaine experienced no fear. He was merely filled with blind rage. He was past caring whether other people in the GLBTQ Library heard him. Blaine wanted David to hear him, loud and clear.

"I let you hit me, fuck other people, treat me like shit because I thought you loved me. You beat the shit out of me and called it love, called it lessons I had to learn. Then you left me broken. You left me, but I put myself back together, piece by piece. I won't let you have any piece of me again. Not ever again."

He was breathing hard now. Looking at David, he wasn't sure what he ever found attractive in him. His blond hair was covering up a bald spot in the back and he was starting to

109

develop jowls. He had stooped shoulders and a fat gut. Blaine was surprised when a realization hit him: David was weak.

Blaine didn't know why it had taken him so long to see this, that David preyed on those that were weaker than him, took everything they had and threw them out like trash when he was done. He had almost taken everything from Blaine, but now it was Blaine that was done.

David's blue eyes were still the same, however, still as cold and unfeeling as they had always been. The difference was that this time, he wasn't afraid of him, or of what David could do. This time, he was ready.

"Are you fucking done?" David asked. "It's time we went home. Get your things."

Blaine stood his ground. "I'm not going anywhere with you."

David's blue eyes blazed with their own cold fire and he reached over the check- out desk to grab Blaine's wrist. "I said, get your fucking things."

"No!" Blaine stood up and grabbed the book David had used as a pretence to see him. He didn't think, but hit David with it. It was a large hardcover, an omnibus edition of the first three books in the *Tales of the City* series. With each smack of the book, Blaine let out a loud "No." All of his hits were aimed at the face, where David had been too afraid to hit him in case someone noticed. It was not a place that Blaine was afraid to hit David.

"NEVER AGAIN!" His screams had reached a fever pitch now but Blaine didn't care. His body was lighter than it had been, as if what was holding him down all this time had finally been lifted. "Never again." Blaine said again.

Hands took hold of Blaine's shoulders and he spun around, the book held high to come down on the person behind him. When Blaine saw that it was Justin, Blaine let out a loud sob and dropped the book with a clunk. Blaine clutched at Justin, pulled him closer and experienced a rush of relief when Justin pulled him closer.

"It's okay, Blaine. It's okay. I've got you and I'm never letting go."

Tears were sliding down his face again, but this time they were tears of relief, of gratefulness. "I know. I know that. Sorry if I lost it."

"You have nothing to be sorry about."

"You're wrong," David said.

They turned and saw him standing there, the patrons of the library looking at all three of them. David's face was bloody and a black eye was already forming. Blood dripped from his face and made him look somehow more inhuman.

"Both of you are going to be very sorry."

When he lunged around the desk towards them, Blaine did the only thing he could think of. He stood in front of Justin and prepared for the blows to come.

Chapter Forty-One

However, the blows never came.

Just as David was about to land his first punch to Blaine's face, a hand reached out and grasped it, twisting the arm, causing David to let out an anguished yelp. The hand had thick fingers tipped in short red nails. The scent of White Diamonds by Elizabeth Taylor hung strongly in the air.

"I simply can't allow you to manhandle my staff like this. Have you no manners? Causing such a fuss?" Ms. Robinson stood a few inches higher than David but she seemed to loom larger than ever above him. "How dare you come in here and threaten sweet Blaine. How dare you."

"He hit me first." David spat out. "He threw the first punch."

"It's true." A regular Blaine knew as Carmondy said. "Blaine did, but this fucker deserved it. I know an abuser when I see one." She pointed at her eyes and then at David. "We all know what you are, don't we everyone?"

The other patrons behind her all nodded.

"He tried to grab hold of Blaine, something about going with him. Hitting him was the smartest thing Blaine could do." The crowd behind them nodded in agreement.

Justin took Blaine's hand. "It was the bravest thing."

Blaine looked at him, saw the love in Justin's eyes "You think I'm brave?"

"The bravest man I know."

Resisting the urge to kiss him right then and there, Blaine just said, "I love you."

"Excuse me!" David said.

They all turned and looked at him. "What is it you want?"

Ms. Robinson asked. She let go of his hand as if he were covered in some sort of a disease; perhaps in a way, he was.

"Aren't you going to call the police?" David asked, almost bellowing.

"They've already been called and should be here any moment to arrest you." Ms. Robinson gave David a small, wry smile.

"Arrest me?! Me? He was the one who assaulted me!"

"Oh, no, my silly little man. You assaulted Blaine, and then Justin. All of the people here will swear to it. You do not harm one of my boys or cause them harm in any way. I will not allow it."

"What the fuck are you talking about, you fucking tranny bastard?" David almost spat. "They aren't your boys! Or did you pop them out of the hole where you used to have a dick?"

Ms. Robinson gave David a wintery glare that put his own to shame. When she spoke, her voice was lower than Blaine had ever heard it before. "What did you say?"

"You heard me. Why did you become a woman? Would no one fuck you as a man?"

Ms. Robinson gave David a little laugh that sounded like glass breaking. Then she pulled her arm back and punched him hard in the face. David's head snapped back and spittle flew from his mouth. Then he flopped to the floor in a heap, out cold.

The library patrons around them all clapped. Ms. Robinson gave them all a little bow. "God that felt good!" She chuckled, "How about applause for the lovely Blaine and his prince charming, Justin!" The patrons all clapped louder.

Ms. Robinson held out her hands, one for Justin and one for Blaine. Together, they all bowed. When they stood again, Blaine leaned in to Ms. Robinson.

113

"But I didn't do anything," he said.

She looked at him with a merry twinkle in her eyes. "Didn't do anything? You went at him like a drag queen when the shoe salesman tries to give her a pair of sensible shoes to wear! I mean, look at him!" She gestured at David, out cold on the floor. "You stood up to your fears. I'd say that's plenty, dear boy." She gave him a kind smile. "Now go out for a drink, you two. You're off shift tonight. Go celebrate your freedom."

Chapter Forty-Two

Mike wasn't sure how this had happened.

He was sitting next to William, naked and covered only with a sheet. Their skin was still slicked with sweat and his heart was still running a mile a minute. He was surprised by how much deeper his attraction to William had become. The world as he knew it had turned upside down and he didn't know what to do.

"You're thinking too much," William said.

"How can you tell I'm thinking too much?"

"You always get this little crease between your eyebrows when you're having a good hard think, or you're trying to beat the next level in Mario Brothers."

Mike warmed further still. "You notice stuff like that?

"I notice everything about you. The way your laugh sounds when it's fake or really happy and genuine. How you always save your favourite portion of a meal for last, how you pretend to read the articles in the newspaper but always turn to the funnies first. You're amazing, Mike. You really are."

Cheeks blushing, Mike leaned in to kiss William. "You are, too." He was silent for a moment, just a beat, but then asked, "So, what happens now?"

"I was thinking we would get married."

Mike laughed. "We already are married."

"Well yes, but we can renew our vows, now that they mean something."

His heart lodging somewhere in his throat, Mike turned to look at William. "What do you mean?"

"Well, now that we're really husbands and not just fuck buddies."

Mike took his time responding but when he did, his voice was cold. "We were never fuck buddies. How could we be when we never slept together? We got married because you said you wanted a partner, not a husband."

"And now I do. I want you and only you. I want all of you."

"You didn't before?" Mike tried to keep calm.

"Michael, listen." William took both his hands in his. "You have to admit the fact that we got married and had never slept together, only sleeping with other people... that was odd, even for two fags. We had an odd relationship and it worked, for a time. Now I'm telling you that I want all of you, that I want to renew our vows because our relationship is stronger."

"Because we finally slept together?"

"No, because we were finally honest with each other about our feelings. You are the only man for me, the only man I could ever want. I want the whole world to know that."

The coldness was gone. All that was left in Mike was a feeling of warmth and heat for this man. "Where have you been all this time?"

"Right here beside you. So will you? Will you marry me, all over again?"

"Nothing would give me more pleasure. Do you want to go to the Justice of the Peace, again?"

"No, this time I want to give you the wedding you deserve. I want it big, outside somewhere, so everyone can come and everyone can see."

Mike laughed. "Just think, I get to tell Nancy he gets to be the flower girl!"

Chapter Forty-Three

Nan wasn't expecting the knock at her door. Normally, if it was one of the boys or Poppy, they would just walk in. Nan went to answer it, wondering who it could be. A wide smile broke out on her face as she saw Romilda through the window.

"Romilda! Honey, what are you doing here? Shouldn't you be at the library?"

Crossing the threshold, she drew Nan into a big hug. "Cordelia, you look lovely as always."

"Oh, you!" She pulled back. "You know that flattery will get you everywhere with me. Did you want a drop of something?"

"I could be tempted."

"Well come in, come in! Don't want you to have an excuse to accuse me of bad manners."

Nan walked towards the kitchen with Romilda following behind her. "What brings you here? Why have you left the library?" She took two glasses down from the cupboard and took out a bottle of red wine from the wine rack. The young ones preferred stronger drinks, but Romilda was a lady; or she was now, at any rate, and that amounted to the same thing.

"Well, it's about Blaine."

Nan turned to look at her, the bottle of wine still in her hand. "What's wrong? Is he all right?"

"He's fine." Romilda sighed. "David showed up."

"Oh." Nan took a breath. "Well, shit." She put the bottle of wine back in the rack and took out the bottle of whiskey instead. "Wine won't do for this. Tell me."

"Well, I don't really know where to begin..."

"The beginning is a good place to start. Tell me

everything."

Romilda sighed but looked thrilled despite the weight of her news. "It was really quite something. I can see why you're so proud of him."

"For fuck's sake, what happened?"

"Well, apparently Blaine and David had some sort of altercation. Blaine got away and went to Justin for comfort. It was so wonderful. He told David where to go. I had to step in, of course."

"Of course you did." Nan took a deep breath. "He really told David where to go?"

"He did. You'll be pleased to know that I gave David what for and a bloody nose to boot. I had him arrested."

Nan let out a loud laugh. It was so good to laugh, freeing. "God, I would have loved to have seen that. I would have paid money. Thank you." She filled a glass with the golden whiskey and handed it to Romilda. "Bottoms up."

Romilda clinked her glass against Nan's. "You won't have to pay. It'll be on the news tonight. The local news showed up just as they were carting David away."

Nan let out another loud hoot of laughter. "Thank you, my friend."

"You're welcome. I'm so glad we've become friends again."

Nan smiled. "Well, admittedly, it took me a while to come around."

"I honestly wondered whether you'd ever forgive me when I told you what I wanted to do."

"I didn't know if I could, but I did in the end. I love you too much, Romilda."

"I love you, too, even though you can be a bit of a bitch sometimes."

"Whore."

"Hag," Nan shot back.

Romilda laughed with a deep baritone. "Well, I must be if he was able to clock me in mere minutes. Seriously though Cordelia, have you told Blaine about his parents?"

Chapter Forty-Four

Nan gave Romilda a searching look.

"I haven't said anything," Romilda replied. "But I really don't see what you're worried about. He has to find out sometime."

"He can't, the truth would ruin him. He thinks I'm his grandmother."

Stepping into Nan's small kitchen, Romilda put her drink down. "I don't understand what the big deal is, Cordelia. After working with him and seeing how wonderful he is, I'm proud to be his father. You should be proud to be his mother."

"I've lied to him for thirty-five years!" Nan said hotly. "How can I just tell him the truth now?"

"Why did you choose to lie to him?

Nan clutched at her glass. "It's complicated."

"Everything in life is complicated, Cordy. You know this. I mean, look at me for Christ's sake!" Romilda let out a loud laugh. "If that's not complicated, I don't know what is."

Snorting a little into her glass of whiskey, Nan took a sip and let out a deep sigh. "Well, it has to do with a few things. Two things, really."

"I know I'm one of them."

"Romilda..."

"No, be honest. What I did to you was inexcusable. By all rights, you shouldn't be talking to me at all. I left you with a baby."

"You didn't know until later. After you told me what you wanted to do, that you were going to Montreal to have the operation done, I was heartbroken. There I was, an almost fifty-year old woman, alone. When I found out I was pregnant,

I didn't know what to do."

"Did you consider... methods other than childbirth?"

"Romy!" Nan was shocked, but it didn't last long. "Of course I did. The doctors all told me I should abort the baby, given my age. But I wanted to keep it."

"Why?"

"Because that baby would be all I had left of you."

There was silence between the two of them for a while. They were both reviewing their memories of that time, Nan knew. Hers flipped past her eyes like a movie, each moment a still from the film she could view frame by frame. When she spoke again, her voice was softer.

"When Blaine was a baby, I looked at all the other mothers and they were so much younger, children themselves really. I looked so much older; I *was* so much older. I was forty-eight when I had Blaine. I knew that by the time Blaine was ready for grade one, I would be fifty-four. By the time he was ready for high school, I would be sixty-two. It seemed easier to pretend, really. Easier for me at the time and, I hoped, easier for him."

"What did you tell him?" Romilda's voice was kind.

Tears began to sparkle in Nan's eyes. "I told him that both of his parents had gone away. That they had left years ago and I had no idea for where, but they had left him with me, so that I could raise him."

"Why did you tell him that? All you had to do was contact me, you knew where I was."

"How could I tell him that his father was now a woman? You were gone and the woman I was had died! What was I supposed to tell him?"

"How about the truth?" said another voice.

121

They both turned. Poppy was standing in the kitchen doorway.

Chapter Forty-Five

Nancy stared at the phone. He was willing it to ring at the same time he was willing it not to. He didn't know what to do.

His mind told him that he was fine, that he was okay with how things had turned out with Devon. His heart, on the other hand, said otherwise. It was breaking and there was only one cure for it.

However, could he let himself love Devon, even knowing what he did? Nancy had always dreamed of a man that would want him and only him. He never imagined falling for someone who made their living fucking other men.

Just as he was about to admit defeat and dial Devon's number, his cell phone rang. Nancy looked at the call display and was scared, terrified, and swooning all at once. His phone showed Devon's phone number on the call display.

With shaking fingers, and an even shakier heart, Nancy took a deep breath and answered the call. "Hello?"

"Nancy! Thank God you answered!"

Despite himself, Nancy was pleased. "I had to eventually. You've filled up my voicemail on my home phone and my cell phone."

"Nancy, please, I need to see you. I need to talk to you. I can't stand how things were left between us."

"I owe you an apology, too. It was wrong of me to try and tell you what to do, to make my love conditional."

"It's okay, Nancy."

"No, it's not. It's not okay. It's not fair of me to tell you what to do, how to live, and only then will I love you. That's wrong. I never should have done that."

Devon was silent for a moment before speaking. "What

changed your mind?"

"I had a talk with my grandmother. She put some sense into me."

"Your grandmother sounds like a smart woman."

Nancy thought of Nan and couldn't help smiling. "Yes, she is."

"So, where do we go from here?"

Nancy took a deep breath, knowing what he had to say. "How about we start over? Some things have to change though."

"I thought it was okay... what'd I do?"

"It is and isn't. But I'm not talking about that. I mean, no more lies and I want you to be proud to be with me, proud of who I am."

"Nancy, I've always been proud of you. How can I not be proud of someone so fabulous?"

"Oh, I bet you say that to all the boys."

"No, usually my mouth is too full of their small cocks to say anything but 'mumble mumble wumble.'"

Nancy couldn't help himself and let out a loud laugh. "Well, at least that's something. You don't have to talk to them."

"No, I want to talk to you."

"Am I making a mistake?"

"I don't think so. Why do you ask?"

"Because I'm frightened of getting hurt." Nancy took a breath. "You really hurt me, Devon. I want to be mean to you, but it just isn't in me right now. But I'm so afraid of seeing you again, of letting you get close."

"Sometimes, the things that frighten us most are the things worth doing. You free tonight? Would you meet me at the coffee house I took you to on our first date?"

124

"Sure."

"There's something I need to tell you but I don't want to do it over the phone. I need to tell you in person. Promise you'll be there?"

"I promise."

Devon let out a breath. "Good, that's good. I can't wait to see you, Nancy."

"Likewise."

Nancy hung up the phone and wondered if he was making a mistake. Only time would tell. Until then, he had a date to get ready for. His phone rang again.

"Nancy, emergency meeting in twenty minutes at The Cabin." It was Justin.

"What's wrong? Is Blaine okay?"

"He's fine, he's with me. Just call the others and be here in twenty minutes, okay?"

"Okay. Thanks Justin, you take care of him."

"I always will."

Nancy hung up the phone and sighed. A queen's work was never done.

Chapter Forty-Six

Devon's heart beat for Nancy.

He hadn't thought this much about a guy in... well, ever. For three days, he hadn't been able to get Nancy out of his head. He couldn't sleep, he couldn't eat. He could only think of Nancy.

His best friend, Rebecca, took one look at him and smiled. "You've got it bad," she said. She dunked a tea bag in hot water. They were in her favourite hangout, The Cloven Hoof, a café that sold coffee, tea, and pastries and displayed work by local artists.

"I've got what bad? My last test results came back clean."

She laughed and slapped his arm. "I'm not talking about anything like that. I'm talking about love."

The very mention of the word caused a hard lump to form in his throat. Swallowing around it, he croaked out, "Love?"

"Sure. You're pale, haven't eaten or slept. Your work is suffering; you haven't taken nearly as many tricks lately as you normally do. So who's the guy and when do I meet him?"

"I don't even know if he'll speak to me anymore." Devon took a sip of his own coffee. It tasted bitter.

"Why? It can't be that bad can it?" Rebecca winked at him. "Just throw on a bit of your charm and he'll be putty in your hands."

"You don't get it. I already fucked up. I don't know how to fix it."

She put down her tea and made Devon put down his coffee, then she took his hands in hers. "All right. Spill."

"There's not much to tell, really. We met, had a connection, then he found out I hooked for a living."

Rebecca grimaced. "Shit, honey, you didn't tell him?"

"Well I did, after I freaked out on him and blew him off for a client. Then he goes and falls in love with me anyway."

"Devon, that's fantastic!"

"It gets worse. He came to tell me he loved me and saw me coming out of the washroom after sucking some guy off."

"Oh honey. That's really bad timing on your part."

"I didn't have anything to do with the timing. Things happen for a reason, right?"

"So what did he say?"

"He told me why he was there, that if I gave up hooking, he'd be all mine."

"So you said yes, of course."

"No... I didn't."

Rebecca stared at him, open mouthed. Then she slapped him hard across the face.

Devon put his hand up to his cheek and looked at her. "What was that for?"

"What was that for? Are you fucking shitting me? A nice man falls in love with you and tells you all you have to do is give up hooking and you tell him what? That hooking is what you do for a living?"

"How else am I going to support myself?"

"Oh, gosh, maybe get a real fucking job like everyone else? You're lucky, damn lucky, you haven't caught something."

"There have been a few close calls," Devon admitted.

"There. Well, at least one of you is showing sense. Find this boy, tell him you love him, as you so clearly do!" She let out an angry snort. "Men! Handed love and what do you do? Walk away!"

"I'm not used to loving men, just fucking them."

"Then maybe it's time you try fucking one you love for a

change, huh?"

The talk still stung, but she'd spoken the truth. Devon could no longer deny that he missed Nancy, that he adored him, that he loved him. After the phone call, Devon felt lighter than he had in a long time. He was going to tell Nancy tonight.

His phone rang and he pressed answer. "Yes?"

"Is this Devon?"

"Yes, who is this please?"

"My name's David. I need the works and I'll pay you double your usual fee."

Devon was shocked. Normally, men tried to bargain with his prices. They never offered him double up front. Guy must be hard up. "Sounds good. When did you want to do this?"

"Tonight," David said.

The guy's voice was cold. Devon could deal with that. He'd dealt with his share of assholes before. "Can't tonight. What other time is good for you?"

"It's tonight or nothing. Take it or leave it. What's it going to be?"

Devon hated himself for wanting to call Nancy and cancel. Seven hundred dollars was nothing to sneeze at. He could pay his whole month's rent with that and have money left to spare.

"So," David said, "what's it going to be?"

Chapter Forty-Seven

Poppy glared at them.

She wasn't just angry for herself, she was more angry for Blaine. She hated it when anyone lied; maybe her rules of decorum were too strict, too old fashioned, but that's the way it was. "How could you lie to Blaine like that?"

Nan was visibly shaken. "Poppy dear, I did what I thought was best at the time."

"And you never thought of sharing the truth with Blaine?"

"No, dear. I couldn't. I was too shattered. After Ernest left and became Romilda, I was too ashamed."

"Well, that should have been cleared up when Blaine came out of the fucking closet!"

"Now, Poppy," Romilda said, "I think you're being too harsh on Cordelia. She did what she thought was best."

"What she thought was best was to raise Blaine with a lie!" She was angry now, but she didn't care. They had to know how wrong they were. "Blaine has wondered all his life who his parents were! Why both of his parents left him! Wondered who he most resembled, who he got his traits from! Don't you realize that? Either of you? Do you feel no shame?"

Poppy walked over to Nan, who backed away from the look in her eyes, but all Poppy did was reach for the bottle of whiskey on the kitchen counter. Raising the bottle to her lips, she took a healthy swig.

"God, that's good."

"Not too much dear, think of the baby," Nan said softly.

"Says the woman who put vodka in my pink lemonade," Poppy said.

Romilda stepped forward as if to protect Nan. "Now, you

listen here, young lady, there's no need to be so mean."

"But don't you see? You were the ones that were mean to Blaine! He's wanted to know about his mom and dad his entire life, and here you both were, watching him grow up and not saying a thing!"

There was silence in the kitchen for a moment before Nan spoke. "She's right, Romilda. She's right. We should have told him. We should have said something to him a long time ago. There was nothing to be ashamed of, only my own hurt."

"I have to know though, why did you get Blaine a job with the woman who was his father?"

"That was at my request," Romilda said. "I'd seen so many pictures, but had never met my son. I wanted to see what kind of a man Cordelia had raised."

"A damn fine one," Poppy said.

"I couldn't agree more," Romilda said proudly.

"So I suppose you're going to tell Blaine now? You'll tell him everything?" Nan's voice shook a little and she hated herself for it, hated herself for the fear she heard in her voice.

"Nope," Poppy said.

"No? You're not going to tell him?" Nan sounded relieved.

"No, you are." Poppy took another swig of the whiskey and turned to leave.

"Where are you going, dear?" Nan asked.

"Muff diving," Poppy said. Romilda, who had just taken a sip of her own whiskey, spit it out in a shower.

As Poppy left, Nan was handing her a rag.

Chapter Forty-Eight

Chuck wasn't sure how any of this had happened.

Sebastian had started ripping off his clothes the moment they got into his apartment. Chuck had never experienced anything like it, this all-consuming need to be touched by another man; that if he didn't get touched everywhere and in between, he would combust. He imagined the combustion would look like a cloud of sparkles, but he could live with that.

Since that night Chuck had waited for Sebastian outside his apartment, they had spent every spare moment together. The most interesting thing to Chuck was that, apart from some heavy make out sessions, they had yet to fuck. It wasn't that Chuck didn't want to; he did very much. However, every time Chuck made a move that could be considered an overture, Sebastian brushed it aside and snuggled closer

Chuck didn't know if it was him, or something he had said. He was going to find out tonight. He had to. Sebastian was driving him crazy with need. He didn't just want Sebastian. Chuck needed him.

He knocked on Sebastian's apartment door, holding a bottle of wine. Sebastian had cooked every night, so bringing by booze was the least he could do. Besides, if he was going to probe Sebastian for his secrets (and hopefully Sebastian himself), he wanted him nice and limber.

The door opened and there stood Sebastian, looking wonderful. Chuck's heart beat just a little faster, his breath coming out just a little rougher. The light hit Sebastian in such a way that he almost looked feminine.

Pulling the door open wider, Sebastian smiled at Chuck.

"Why hello. You're early."

"I didn't want to be late for a very important date, you know."

"I like that about you. Your mother must have raised you to be a gentleman." Closing the door with a short laugh, Sebastian turned and caught Chuck's mouth with his own. His tongue dipped inside and explored, and Chuck's own tongue explored back.

Sebastian tasted of cloves and smoke, like a good red wine. He tasted so good that Chuck almost forgot what was on his mind. He broke the kiss and pretended not to see the hurt look that was there and gone so quickly on Sebastian's face.

"Can I pour you a glass?"

"Please do. You know the way." He grinned at Chuck, and Chuck's heart skipped a beat.

Chuck went to the kitchen and got two wine glasses from the cupboards. He poured two glasses of the deep red wine, its scent reminding him so much of how Sebastian tasted. They clinked glasses and Chuck took a healthy swig of wine, trying to quell his nervousness. Sebastian sensed it right away though.

"What's wrong, Charles?"

"I...I've been meaning to talk to you," he said. "I want to talk to you."

A pained look crossed Sebastian's features. "This doesn't sound good."

"It's not you, well maybe it is, but I wanted to talk to you."

"So talk," Sebastian said gently.

"Why won't you make love to me?"

"This from the man who wants to fuck all the time."

"I mean it. You tell me you love me, I love you. So it's not just fucking, it's making love. Why haven't we done that yet?

We've been dating for a while now and the only time I saw you mostly naked was at the bathhouse. What gives? Do you not find me attractive?"

"God yes, of course I do!" He took Chuck's hands in his own and squeezed them. "I find you irresistible."

"But you won't sleep with me."

"It's... it's complicated. My junk doesn't work like yours does."

"Hey, it's all good if you have impotency problems. That's why they invented Viagra, right?"

"No, Charles, it's not that... God, I should have told you before now, I should have said something."

"You're married to a woman, you love someone else, you're actually an opera singer in disguise."

Sebastian took one look at Chuck and burst out laughing "Where did you get any of that from?"

Chuck let out his own chuckle. "Well, you're not saying much, so I thought I'd see if I could guess your secret. What's wrong?"

Closing his eyes for a second, Sebastian looked away. When he looked back at Chuck, he was crying. "There's no easy way to say this, so I'm just going to say it. Charles, I'm trans."

"Like a transient? Honey, no one is born here, everyone comes to the city. "

Letting out a nervous laugh, Sebastian touched Chuck's cheek softly, almost as if it was the last time he would do so.

"No, turkey. "I'm transgender. I was assigned female at birth.""

Chapter Forty-Nine

There was silence in the kitchen.

Sebastian looked at Chuck and pleaded with his eyes. "Say something," he said. "Say anything. Tell me what you're feeling."

Chuck was in a shock so intense that all he could do was look at Sebastian, really look at him. He could only see the man he fell in love with, could only see Sebastian. "You're not a woman. I would know it."

Blushing, Sebastian poured more wine into each of their glasses. "Thanks, that's quite the compliment, all things considered."

"But you're not a woman."

"I was, though. I'm who I was always meant to be."

"You're having me on. As jokes go, it's a pretty fucking sick one."

"This isn't a joke, Charles. I'm not joking. Here."

He put down his glass of wine and came closer. Chuck was surprised by how much he still wanted to put his hands on Sebastian, to taste him, even if this was freaking him out a little bit.

Sebastian began to unbutton his shirt.

"What are you doing?"

"Showing you that what I said is true."

"Sebastian, you don't have to do this."

"Yes, I do."

He took off his shirt and let it fall to the floor. He stood there in the light of the kitchen and Chuck couldn't help but be turned on by how great he looked. Muscled pecs covered in a soft down of chest hair.

"See?" Sebastian said. "Do you see the scars?"

He pointed to right below the pectoral muscles and there, running along the edges of both of them, were thin red lines. Chuck ran his fingers along each of them and Sebastian shivered at his touch.

"There's more." Sebastian said. He started to undo his pants.

"What are you doing?"

Sebastian stopped and looked at Chuck, his eyes large and round. "If I'm going to sleep with you, be with you completely, I want you to know everything about me. I want you to know all of me."

"Stop this, Sebastian. This is just a sick joke. "

A hurt look crossed Sebastian's face. "I'm not joking. I'm telling you the truth. The whole truth."

"But you're a man! You're clearly a man! I've felt your cock growing hard when we make out and everything! Everyone knows that a tranny guy can't have a working cock!"

The hurt look deepened. "The clitoris acts like a penis, you know. The testosterone helps do the rest."

"But you are a man! I'm only attracted to men! Not trannies! I would know if you were a tranny! Why are you telling me this?"

"Because I wanted you to know all of me."

Chuck looked at this gorgeous man, this wonderful man that he loved with all of his heart and could have sworn that it broke a little. "I thought I already did."

He left as quickly as he could, leaving Sebastian looking shattered in his kitchen. As he was taking the stairs down to the first floor, his cell phone beeped.

Chuck answered. "Yeah?"

"Honey, get over to The Cabin, now. Something's up with

Blaine." It was Nancy.

"Shit, is he okay?"

"I think so, Justin's with him. Ten minutes, okay?"

"I'm on my way."

Chuck ended the call and exited the stairwell into the darkness of dusk. He went to his car and took one look back at Sebastian's apartment.

He was standing in his apartment window, watching him.

Feeling like an asshole, Chuck got in his car and drove away.

Chapter Fifty

Nancy was almost at The Cabin when his cell phone rang.

Looking at the number, he felt a moment of pure happiness. He clicked answer. "Hey, handsome! I meant to call you, is it okay if we do a late dinner? Something's come up with one of my friends. You know Blaine? Something's up, another gay emergency that this royal has to clean up."

"Oh, that's good," Devon said.

Nancy gave his phone a sardonic look even though he knew that Devon couldn't see him. "Good? Honey, something's wrong. I'm going to go sort it out and then we can go to dinner."

"I...I was calling to cancel, actually."

Nancy stopped walking. "What do you mean you were calling to cancel?"

"Look, it's not that I don't want to go to dinner. I do."

"Then come to dinner with me, fuckwad! What's so hard with that? All I'm asking for is a half hour, it won't take that long."

"It's not that... Nancy, something's come up. I can't meet you tonight."

Nancy's heart plummeted to the pavement in little pieces. "You mean something will come up, eventually."

Devon huffed. "Look Nancy, I don't want to do this, but he offered me a lot of money."

"That's wonderful, Devon. Enjoy your evening." He tried to keep the coldness out of his voice but wasn't successful.

"Look, Nancy, David offered me a lot of money, enough to pay my rent this month and then some. There was no way I could say no"

"Yes there was. How about telling him you had plans with me!?"

"Clarence, don't be like this."

"I'll be any way I damn well please!" He was practically screaming now, but he didn't care. He wanted Devon to eat his heart, every piece of it, through the telephone. "You're telling me you'd rather fuck some guy you don't know, rather than be with me?"

"Clarence, don't be like this," Devon said again.

"My name is Nancy, you cock-wielding motherfucker."

"Hey, you were the one who told me that you were trying to be more open about what I do for a living!"

"That's before you brushed me aside to fuck some guy!" Something clicked in Nancy's head. "Hold on a minute, did you say his name was David?"

"Yeah."

"Blond hair and cold blue eyes?"

"I don't know, I haven't met him yet."

"Devon, I've got a bad feeling about this. Even if you're going to treat me like shit, trust me when I tell you this guy is bad news."

"You don't even know if it's the same guy."

"I do. I have a bad feeling."

"Is that all you have to go on?"

"You must have it too. You wouldn't have even told me about him, just brushed me off like before."

"You know I wouldn't have done that."

"I do. You did it before, what's to stop you from doing it again?" Fresh tears poured down Nancy's cheeks and he was careful not to step on the pieces of his heart that littered the ground.

"You don't even know me!" Devon's anger was instant,

giving rise to the notion that he was angrier at himself than at Nancy.

"No, you're right. I don't." He took a deep breath. "Fuck you, Devon. Fuck you and David. Don't contact me again."

He hung up, feeling as if he was closing a book on a chapter that had barely even begun before it was over. Wiping his tears on his sleeve, Nancy pushed open the door to The Cabin. He saw them already sitting at a table: Blaine and Justin, Mike, William and Chuck. Only Chuck looked exactly how he felt. Squaring his shoulders, he walked up to the table.

"Who's gonna buy this bitch a Mai Tai?" he asked.

Chapter Fifty-One

Poppy hesitated. She had been doing this a lot lately.

Normally she was a take-charge kind of woman, but ever since River Moon Falls, AKA Connie Collins, had come into her life, that part of her had taken a back-seat. She had changed a bit of that when she kicked Connie's ass out of her apartment, but she had lost part of herself.

Hence why she was standing in front of a bar, pregnant and alone. She rubbed her stomach absently. She had started showing recently. One day there had been nothing to see and now there was this baby bump. Poppy didn't know why people thought baby bumps were sexy: it just made her feel fat. However, she didn't hate her baby bump. Poppy wanted to protect it.

Sure, she was going into a lesbian bar where there was tons of smoke and booze, and she was more than likely going to have a white wine spritzer. But you only live once, right?

The Delphic Oracle was one of three lesbian bars in the city, and the only one worth going to. There was the Hairy Clam down on 6th and Kent and then there was the Dirty Girl out in the east end, but both of those bars catered to a rough crowd. Poppy was more of a beer-and-martinis kind of girl.

She'd known some women who had called her a lipstick lesbian. What was the problem with looking pretty? She wasn't a hippie, hated granola, wasn't into leather or riding a motorcycle. A lot of lesbians loved to assert themselves in a man's world, doing what the man did or was able to do.

Not Poppy. She was quite happy being a woman and was attracted to other women, thank you very much. She wasn't into whips, chains, strap-ons, or any of that bullshit. What had ever happened to good, old-fashioned sex?

I mean, sure, she liked a bit of role-playing, but essentially just wanted to fall into a person she felt everything for. It had started out that way with Connie, but when Connie had returned from the women's retreat, she had been a different person, all angsty and angry.

Wading into a crowd of people, Poppy found her way to the bar. She saw Agnes, her favourite bartender, was on duty tonight. She had gorgeous tits and beautiful red hair teased a mile high. Unfortunately, she was straight. Agnes didn't mind if the ladies wanted to look at her breasts, she said it got her good tips.

When Agnes saw her, she smiled. "Honey! Long time, no see! How you doing?"

"Fine. Here for a drink. What do you have that's non-alcoholic?" Poppy only shuddered slightly when she said this.

"Oh my God." Agnes looked her up and down. "Fresh skin, rosy glow, brightness in your eyes. So the bitch was telling the truth."

Poppy didn't have to ask who the bitch was or what Agnes was referring to. She knew that Connie would have been in and everyone would know all about what happened. The gay community was notoriously small, almost incestuous. It was near impossible to sleep with someone who didn't have a connection to one of your past forays. Being a gay man was worse; those fuckers would sleep with anything.

"So she's been in?" was all that Poppy said.

"Yeah, but none of us believed it. I mean, it's one thing to kick that bitch out, good for you, honey! But the reason? That you were preggers? I didn't believe it. Who's the father?"

"Justin Carmichael."

"Justin? Oh my God honey, your baby will be gorgeous!

How far along are you?"

"Three months." Poppy patted her baby bump.

"Well, not too long now and you'll be a mom of one of the most beautiful baby girls EVER."

"How do you know the baby will be a girl?"

Agnes shrugged. "I just have a feeling." Her face paled. "Oh shit." She was looking at something behind Poppy.

Turning around, Poppy cursed her luck. Standing behind her, with arms crossed and an angry expression stitched on her face, was Connie.

Chapter Fifty-Two

"What the fuck are you doing here?" Connie nearly shrieked.

"Hello to you too, Connie."

"It's River Moon Falls!"

"Honey, that's not your name, that's a name for dress-up, for make-believe. You're no more in touch with your spirit than you are with your uterus."

Connie was spitting, she was so angry. "That name was given to me by Elder Leeana and was told to her by the Goddess!"

"Too bad she didn't call you 'Rock Paper Scissors,'" Poppy said. She heard Agnes laugh. Connie, though, looked enraged.

"You can't mock me! You fucking straight piece of shit! You and your fucking whore of a baby!"

Poppy held a hand up. "Hold up. The baby hasn't even had sex yet, so I have no idea if she'll be a whore. And it's unfair to judge straight people with me as their champion. I'm a dyke and proud of it."

"Hear, hear," Agnes said.

"Stop mocking me! You ridiculed me and made me worthless when you kicked me out!"

"Funny, you do a good job of being worthless on your own. I didn't have to do anything."

"You fucking bitch! This is all your fault!"

"Connie, it's not my fault that you're so fucking ugly and uptight. You really have to do something about your anger management issues, you know. Take that stick out of your ass. It'll be easier to walk."

Letting out a yell of rage, Connie slapped her hard across

the face. The sound of the slap was loud even above the music that thumped through the speakers. Poppy, who had never been hit before, put a hand to her cheek and looked at a woman that she thought she had known.

Connie was red-faced, and her mouth was drawn in a tight grimace that showed her teeth. She looked like an enraged rhino. She pulled back her fist and Poppy, who was staring at this unknown animal woman, knew that Connie meant to punch her in the stomach.

She heard Agnes scream behind her and tried to protect herself but knew that there was nothing she could really do. She used her words to fight, not her fists. Poppy turned away, shielding her stomach. She prepared for the punch, but it never came.

Another woman, with spiky grey hair and glasses, pushed Connie at the last moment, before the punch would have landed. "You leave her alone!" the woman said. She was shorter than Poppy, but no less commanding because of her height. Her eyes burned like two hot coals behind her glasses. "Shame on you for attacking another person, let alone a pregnant one! Have you no decency?"

Connie lay there, on the ground of the bar where she had fallen. A crowd of people stood in a circle around them and they looked at Connie with disgust. "She ruined my life! I had everything and she took it from me!"

The woman snorted. "I'd say you're doing a really good job of fucking up your own life without her help. Now get out of here, before I call the police."

Agnes called over the bouncers and they picked Connie up and carried her from the bar. Poppy tried to suppress a smile but couldn't. The smile grew wider when the woman with the spiky hair and glasses turned toward her.

"You okay?"

"I'm fine. I was a little worried there for a moment, but you saved me."

"It was a pleasure to save someone so beautiful."

Poppy was charmed despite herself. She held out her hand. "I'm Poppy."

"I know." She held out her own hand and took hold of Poppy's. A spark of electricity passed between them. "I'm Dava."

Chapter Fifty-Three

Blaine looked up as Nancy approached the group. He could tell that Nancy had been crying. No amount of makeup could hide the puffy cheeks, the red eyes. Knowing Nancy as well as he did, Blaine knew that it took a lot to make him cry.

He stood up and hugged Nancy. "You okay?"

"Never been better."

"You sure? You've been crying."

"I know I have and I'm not ready to talk about it yet. Let me pick up the pieces of my heart and then I'll be all fabulous again and I'll tell you all about it. We're here for *you,* honey. What happened?"

"It was nothing..." Blaine said.

"It wasn't nothing," Justin cut in. "David was in the GLTBQ Library."

"What!" Nancy said. "That fucker! How did he find you?"

"He was waiting outside the call centre for me. He said he forgave me and it was okay to go back to him. I told him to fuck off, that he didn't own me, and then went to the library. He followed me there."

"That motherfucking son of a bitch!" Nancy almost screamed. "You just wait until I get my hands on him, I'll wring his neck with his Rapunzel-like hair and make him choke out quarters!"

They all looked at Nancy. Blaine could tell his heart was breaking. "Nancy, what happened? Was it Devon?"

"Of course it was motherfucking Devon! He blew me off again 'cuz some guy offered him a ton of cash. Like money is more important than me."

"Well, he is a hooker," Mike said "I hope he's worth it.

Most of them just blow you for sixty and let you fuck them for one hundred."

William gave Mike a sage look. "How would you know this?"

"Hey, you meet some interesting people at the bathhouses."

"Well, it doesn't matter. I'm motherfucking priceless!" Nancy snapped his fingers.

"How much money was it?" Chuck asked.

"He didn't say. Probably a thousand or something."

"No gay man is that good," Chuck replied.

"Look, it doesn't matter. I'm priceless, I'm worth more than any sum of money, and he should know that!"

"We do, Nancy, we do," Blaine said. He didn't know what else to say.

"But I love him!" Nancy said, almost screaming again. "I fucking love him! I thought I would be okay with him hooking, but I just can't do it, it's me or no one else, not all kinds of guys. To make matters worse, I think he's getting together with David tonight."

This ran a chill through Blaine's heart. "How do you know for sure? Did you see a picture?"

"No honey, I have no idea, but I just got this bad feeling, like something awful is going to happen."

"Wooooo!" William said. "Spooky."

"Honey, you know my feelings are bang-on."

"It's true. When George and Kyle broke up because Kyle had fallen in love with a woman, Nancy called it," Mike said.

"Okay, so one time."

"Nope, all the time," Mike replied. "He called it when Nan actually had pneumonia that year instead of just a cold, knew that Poppy would have enough of A River Runs Through Her eventually."

William rolled his eyes. "Anyone would have enough of that trumped up bitch eventually. I mean, come on, did you meet her?"

"Okay, then, Mr. Smarty Pants. How's this: you're getting married to Mike again and Chuck is heartbroken"

There was a moment's silence. "How did you know? We haven't said anything yet?" William said.

"Well, if you must know, I saw your new rings from across the table and anyone could tell that Chuck is slumped down in the dumps. Can't you guys? I mean look at him? What gives, Chuck? Tell Auntie Nancy all about it."

Chapter Fifty-Four

"I let him go," Chuck said.

Then he did something that no one was prepared for, he burst into tears. They rolled down his cheeks fast, in great drops that he didn't bother wiping away. They were all staring at him, open-mouthed. He had never cried over a man before.

"Honey, what's wrong?" Nancy wiped away his own tears. "What happened?"

Chuck looked at all of them, his friends, his family. Hopefully they would understand. "He was a woman."

"I'm sorry, what now? He was a what?" Nancy said.

"Sebastian told me that he was born a woman." The words hung in the air for a moment, the silence around them almost thick enough to cut through.

"Is that why you left him?" Blaine said.

Chuck nodded. "He should have told me. He should have told me."

"Wait, Sebastian is a trans male?" Justin asked.

"Yes."

"So what's your problem?"

Chuck dried his eyes. "What do you mean?"

"Well, what do you see when you look at him?"

Thinking about it for a moment, Chuck answered: "I see only him."

"You said him. You only think of him as a man."

"Yes."

"So what's the problem? Why are you overreacting? He trusted you with his biggest secret, something that probably incredibly hard for him to share, and you what? Ran out of the apartment as fast as you could? Why?"

"Because he's a tranny!"

"No, I don't think that's it," Justin said.

"Where are you going with this? Can't you see how broken up he is?"

"Hear me out. Chuck, aren't you the one that fucks anything that moves?"

"Hey, now." Nancy wagged a finger at him.

"Well, I do resemble that comment a little," Chuck said.

"And now you've found the one guy you want to fuck more than anything else, but more than that, you're in love with him."

"Yeah? So?"

"So that's what you find terrifying. If the fact that he was trans made any difference to you, you'd refer to him as she or it or whatever. But you refer to Sebastian as a guy."

"Because he is."

"So then him being trans isn't the problem, is it? It's because you want to be with him and only him."

Chuck stood up. "You're wrong!"

"Am I? I don't think so."

"I'll prove it to you, I'll fucking prove it." Without even having a drop to drink, he strode out of the bar.

"Where's he going?" William asked.

"To fuck anything that moves at the bathhouse, I suspect," Blaine replied.

Nancy shook his head. "He won't get very far. That boy has it bad." He turned to Justin. "How'd you know?"

"If he was angry over the transgender thing, he'd be angry. Instead, he was acting sad and depressed. Made sense to me."

Nancy gave Justin a once-over. "Oooh, honey, you're good. Blaine, you hold on to this one or I may just have a go at him." He reached out and patted Justin's hand. "Now, for goodness' sake honeys, someone get me a Mai Tai. Then we can figure out what to do about the David situation."

Chapter Fifty-Five

Devon knocked on the door for apartment 1300. He heard the locks disengage and the door opened. Standing there was one of the ugliest men that Devon had ever seen, and he'd seen his fair share of ugly men.

"Took you long enough to get here," the man said.

Devon had never seen eyes that were so cold – the blue looked as if it contained chunks of ice. "David?"

"Of course I'm David. I wouldn't have answered my door if I was someone else, would I?"

His tone was harsh. There were also a number of bruises on his face, and his nose looked as if it might be broken. "What happened to your face?"

"I'm paying for fucking, not fucking questions."

"Can I come in then?"

"No, it's me who'll be coming in you." He stepped aside to let Devon enter.

Stepping across the threshold, Devon had some misgivings, which had never happened before. Sure, he'd been with a lot of rough guys, but there was something different about this guy, something not quite right.

However, the thought of money drew him like the cart before the horse. Ignoring his gut feeling to get out now and run, Devon walked further into David's apartment. David was already taking off his clothes.

"Little eager, aren't you?" Devon said jokingly.

"I don't pay you for wisecracks or jokes. Now strip."

Devon followed David to his bedroom and began taking off his clothes. David was even more unattractive with his clothes off than on. He had a large belly, whether from overeating or booze, he didn't know. It was made to look even bigger than it was by how small everything else about his body was: stick arms, twig legs, and a small, almost deflated, chest. Even his dick was small. There was a scar running along his abdomen, from his ribs to his belly button. David saw him starting at it.

"What? Never seen a fucking scar before?"

"No, it's not that, it's jus-"

"I gave him back as he gave me. Fucking Blaine."

Devon's insides froze. "Blaine?

"Yeah, fucking Blaine. Do you know him, the little pussy? Fucker got uppity one night after I taught him a lesson and pushed me into a glass cabinet. Broke all over the fucking place and I ended up with a piece of the fucking glass in my side. I made him pay, though."

As David spoke to him about making Blaine pay, he grew hard. Devon shook his head, wondering how sick in the head you had to be to get hard or excited over hurting someone else.

"Something fucking wrong?"

"No, it's just..."

"Do you want your money or not?"

"I do. Speaking of which, I usually take payment up front."

"You'll get your money when I'm satisfied. Only then. "

Devon swallowed and went over to David. That feeling of unease was screaming at him to get out, to run, to flee, but the thought of the money kept him there, kept him going closer.

David grabbed him and threw him on the bed in one swift motion. For a scrawny guy, he sure had strength. *It's because his insides are made of ice*, Devon thought. David began trying to push his cock into Devon without any lubricant. Devon hadn't heard the snap of a condom going on and tried to get up off his hands and knees.

A hand grabbed his hair and pushed him back down. "You stay where I tell you."

"I won't do anything without you wearing a condom. Those are my rules. No glove, no love. You know what kind of world we live in." Devon hated that his voice sounded so weak.

"You don't get to tell me what to do! If I want to fuck you bareback, I'll fuck you bareback! I'll fuck you any way I want for the money I'm paying you!"

Devon got up and moved away from him. He turned to face David and saw how angry he looked, how mean and little he looked. Devon realized he had made the wrong choice.

"I'm sorry, I have to go. You keep your money, this was a mistake."

"Damn right it was."

That's when David hit him. The blow came to the side of his head and he fell back on the bed. Another punch and this one hit his jaw. Devon heard bone crack.

"Fucking whore, think you're better than me? Think you are? Think I was going to even fucking pay you?"

David grabbed Devon by the ankles and pulled him off the bed. He tried to kick out, tried to force David off him, to back away, but then David gave him another punch to the face and he saw stars.

Devon heard David rummaging for something in the corner of the room. Still, he tried to get up, to gather his clothes, to get up, to do anything except lie there. He heard the whistle through the air as something hit him in the back, causing pain and heat to blossom there like stars.

Another blow caught him in the ribs and Devon realized what David was hitting him with. It was a baseball bat. It whistled again and pain bloomed along his legs. There was one final blow to his head, David's fist connecting with his skull, and then Devon was down on the ground.

As darkness began to claim him amongst a sea of stars, Devon's last thought was of Nancy.

Chapter Fifty-Six

Approaching The Caveman Room, Chuck tried to ignore the guilt.

It raged through him. He was consumed by it. Almost afraid that he would find Sebastian inside, Chuck opened the door and went in.

Joe was on the front desk. He actually smiled when he saw Chuck. "Hey stranger! Long time, no see! Two weeks must be a record for you." He gave Chuck a roguish grin that he would have found cute under normal circumstances. Now it just reminded him of Sebastian's grin, his supple lips, his smile with a flash of white teeth.

Putting his money on the counter, Chuck grabbed a towel. "Yeah, well, there's a first time for everything."

"Hey, it's all good. Been meaning to talk to you. You know that guy you left with the last time you were here?"

His spine stiffening, Chuck tried to keep his tone neutral. "Yeah?"

"Well, you know what he is, right?"

"An international spy? A man of mystery?"

"Well, you got the mystery part right and he's not really a man. He's a tranny man. He's dick isn't even real."

Chucks fists clenched. "He is so a real man."

"Hey, man, take it easy. I just wanted you to be aware of where you're sticking your dick."

"I haven't stuck it anywhere yet!"

"Well, that's a good thing. She-male couldn't get it up, huh?"

Chuck was surprised by how quickly the anger came. He reached across the desk and grabbed Joe by the collar. He pulled him nearly two feet off the ground, bringing him close enough so that Chuck could see how afraid Joe was. Joe's eyes were like dinner plates in the centre of his face.

"You listen to me. Sebastian is ten times the man you are. Don't you ever forget that or I'll punch your fucking teeth right out of your mouth. You ever say anything else again, I'll kill you."

Joe held up his hands in surrender. "Hey, Chuck, I didn't mean anything by it, honest, I thought you didn't know."

"Yeah, well..." Chuck released Joe, letting him fall back behind the counter. Taking his towel, he went to the locker room to get changed.

When he went inside, he saw that it was in full swing. There were several guys in the locker room, and they all looked at him as he entered. They were in various stages of undress, some of them playing with their hard cocks. Chuck realized that he felt sorry for them, and for him, as he had been one of them.

Picking out a locker, Chuck began to unbutton his shirt. He stopped when he remembered when he'd last worn it. It was when Sebastian had taken him to ride on the pink pony on the merry-go-round. It had been washed since then, but he could swear that he could still smell some of Sebastian's cologne. It was a light, spicy scent that made him instantly hard.

"Now that's what I like to see."

Chuck came out of his reverie to find a naked man staring at him. "Sorry? What?"

"You're not even undressed and you're hard." The man pointed to the erection in Chuck's jeans.

"Yeah, so?"

"So you're not even naked yet and you're ready to play.

Why don't I help you get those pants off, and I can start sucking your dick."

Looking at the man, Chuck wondered if he had ever looked like this. He was slight but well built, a sheen of sweat and moisture covering his skin, but he looked so fucking desperate, so needy.

Chuck realized right then that he didn't want anyone else but Sebastian. Saying nothing, he left the locker room and ran out of The Caveman Room.

He had never prayed before, but as he ran to his car and sped out of the parking lot, he prayed to God that Sebastian would forgive him.

Chapter Fifty-Seven

Poppy raised her glass of non-alcoholic beer and took a sip.

Dava had brought it to the table with a grin. "I hope you don't mind, I took the liberty of getting you some alcohol-free beer. If you can't have the buzz, you can still have the taste."

Poppy thought for a moment. "How'd you know I was pregnant when Connie was about to hit me?"

"Connie, of course. She's been bitching to anyone who'll listen about her skank of an ex- girlfriend who got herself pregnant. Sees it as a personal insult that you got pregnant on your own with a guy, rather than with her and a turkey baster."

Poppy barked out a mouthful of beer and a mouthful of laughter. She wiped her mouth on her sleeve and smiled at Dava. "So everyone knows, huh?"

"Yes, but no one holds it against you. Many would have done the same thing." She reached out and wiped a drop of beer that still rested on Poppy's chin. Giving Poppy a wicked grin, she licked the beer off her finger. "Mmm, tastes good."

Blushing, Poppy raised the glass again and took a sip, unsure as to whether Dava was referring to her or the beer. "So, what are you here for tonight?" It was usually a safe question. You either found out if the woman was clingy, or crazy as a loon.

For her part, Dava didn't strike her as a loon or as particularly clingy. She shrugged. "What is any woman looking for?"

"Sanity? A big house? A strap-on with purple sparkles?" Poppy joked.

"How about honesty, affection, and love?" She took a sip

from her wine glass. "Those seem to be lost things, though."

"Lost things? They aren't lost."

"Says the woman who had sex with a man when she was a lesbian in a committed relationship."

Poppy clinked her glass against Dava's. "Touché."

"So why did you do it? Do you mind if I ask?"

"No, I don't mind. Not really."

"You can tell me to butt the fuck out if you want to. Lord knows I would."

Despite just meeting her, Dava opened up something in her. Looking into her hazel-coloured eyes, Poppy felt only warmth and openness. The words just came out of her and she let them, not wanting to hold them back.

"I wanted to be loved, you know? Just once in my life, I wanted a bit of love, only if it was just for an evening. I was so alone."

"You had Connie..." Even Dava didn't sound too sure about that.

"She had her career. I was a convenience. I was there, a wall dressing. I wanted someone to really see me, just for a moment. That's all I wanted. Just a moment. You ever been with someone but been alone? Do you know what that's like?"

Dava nodded. "I was with my husband for twenty years. I always wanted woman, was attracted to them, but you do what's expected of you, right? Johnson was a cold SOB, but he gave me three sons that I love more than anything, even if he was a dick. When I had had enough, I left him. My sons were all grown and I was free to be who I wanted, needed to be." She paused. "I know exactly what that's like."

Poppy wasn't sure why she said it but the words once again came out of her mouth without warning. "Do you want to ditch this place and go out for dinner?"

Chapter Fifty-Eight

Nancy was downing his fifth Mai Tai when his cell phone rang.

Looking down at his phone, he saw Devon's number. He clicked answer. "Listen dipshit, you need to go fuck yourself good and hard with a mace, okay motherfucker? You aren't getting anywhere near my body when you've been near somewhere else's." Nancy knew he was being vulgar, but it wasn't the worst he had ever said. Still, the Mai Tai's helped.

Instead of Devon's deep smoky voice, there was the sound of crying.

"I'm sorry, who is this? Devon, are you okay?"

A woman answered. "I'm with Devon now. This is his friend, Rebecca."

"Who are you, honey? Why are you calling from Devon's phone?" Cold fear ran down Nancy's spine. He knew he wasn't going to like what he heard next.

"There's been an accident." Rebecca choked back a sob.

That cold fear turned into a flood. "What happened?" Nancy's quiet voice got everyone's attention. Mike, William, Blaine and Justin all looked at him.

"He was seeing one of his clients. I was supposed to pick him up for sushi afterwards and I found him..." She started sobbing again and each sob was a pull at Nancy's heart for a man he had hated with every fibre of his being only a moment before.

"Where are you, Rebecca? Which hospital?"

"The Pinecrest General Hospital. He's asking for you. I keep asking if he's okay and all he says is your name. We're in Room 432."

"I'll be right there."

Nancy hung up the phone, his hands shaking. He looked up at the guys, and was surprised to find himself crying. "That was Devon's friend. He's had an accident. He's in the hospital."

"Let's go," Blaine said. "We'll drive you."

"Guys, I don't know what to do. He's been asking for me. What do I do?"

"You go to him, of course," Justin said. "We'll take you."

Nancy, Blaine, and Justin said goodbye to Mike and William, and Justin promised to update them on what was going on. Nancy was numb as Blaine helped him into the car before getting into the passenger seat. Nancy sat in the back and wondered how it had come to this.

"What did she say happened?" Blaine asked

"She just said that he had been with a client and she had found him. She didn't say what had happened to him."

"It was David then," Blaine said.

"We don't know for sure that it was the same David." Justin said. "We have no way of knowing that; let's not jump to any conclusions."

"I know it was him," Nancy said. "I got a bad feeling. It's too coincidental, like something out of a bad movie script."

"We have no proof that it was him," Justin said.

"You don't know David," Blaine said. "It would be just like him to find someone that has a connection to one of us and hurt him, just for sport."

"So what do we do if it is David that did whatever to him?" Justin said.

"Oh, that's easy." Nancy spoke from quietly from the back seat. "We'll hurt him, like he's hurt us."

No one had a reply for this.

When they arrived at the hospital, Nancy shoved his door

open and ran inside. Justin and Blaine had to run to catch up. They came to the room and found Nancy in the doorway, frozen.

Devon lay in a hospital bed. His face was a mass of bruises and one of his eyes had closed over. His nose was broken and there were tubes of every imaginable sort running from his arms.

He had casts on one of his arms and both of his legs. Blood had leaked into the bandages, making Devon look like some sort of walking Rorschach test. Nancy stood frozen in the doorway, but he looked back at Justin and Blaine.

"What I said before?" Nancy said. "We won't just hurt him. I'm gonna motherfucking kill the bastard." The words came out in a hiss and he nodded to Blaine as if to put a period at the end of his words.

Then, his shoulders squared and his head held high, he stepped into the hospital room and went to the man he loved.

Chapter Fifty-Nine

Poppy didn't know what she was doing.

That was happening a lot lately; from deciding to keep the baby, to getting rid of Connie, to standing up to Nan. She had become a different person, one of purpose and intent. She wondered where this woman had been and why she had stayed quiet for so long. Poppy knew that the woman had always been there, hiding under the surface of her skin. It only took having another life growing inside of her to bring it out.

Well, that wasn't entirely true. The woman she had become had always been there. She had been a bossy child and had always gotten her own way. She just wondered when she had stopped listening to her.

Now the woman she had become wanted to know more about Dava. It had been so long since she had been attracted to anyone that she had forgotten what it felt like. Poppy sat across from Dava, little butterflies running around in her stomach. Poppy wasn't sure if this was due to the baby or indigestion, but she was pretty sure that this was the beginnings of attraction, or what she could remember of it anyway.

Dava's hazel eyes sparkled behind her glasses. "What's going on in that head of yours?"

"Huh?"

"I've been talking for five minutes and you've been miles away."

"What? Oh God, I'm sorry. You must think I'm an idiot."

"Not at all. You've got a lot on your mind."

"What did I miss while you were talking?"

"Oh, nothing, I just told you my plans to take over the

world, the perfect recipe for non-sticky rice, how to cure the world from debt. Nothing major."

Poppy let out a laugh that was close to a snort. "Sorry I missed all that. Can we start again?"

"Sure, but we already have. I know you've got a lot on your mind and it's okay. Really." Dava put a hand out across the table and took one of Poppy's in her own.

Her hand was warm to the touch and Poppy was surprised by the fact that she wanted to feel her hands all over her. She gave her head a shake. "Why are you being so nice to me?"

Tilting her head to the left, Dava gave her a look that was half sadness, half openness. "You haven't known very many kind women, have you?"

Poppy shook her head. "No. I haven't."

"Well, not to toot my own horn, but you couldn't have met a better woman than me."

"Oh, that's modest."

"Indeed. I can fix a car with the best of men but can also whip up a lovely beef Wellington. I'm comfortable in jeans and a t-shirt most of the time, but every now and again I like to dress up. I look hot in a miniskirt."

"I don't doubt that." She blushed and took a drink of water. When the waitress brought their food, Poppy was happy to have something to distract herself with for a bit. She kept stealing glances at Dava though, afraid Dava would realize she was crazy and bolt.

"I'm not going to run, you know."

"What do you mean?"

"You keep looking at me like a deer caught in the headlights of a pickup. I'm not going anywhere unless you want me to. Who hurt you so badly that you'd be frightened of someone who treats you kindly?"

Shaking her head again, Poppy said, "You don't want to know."

"Of course I do, otherwise I wouldn't have asked."

Poppy gave Dava a shrewd look. "Can I ask you something?"

"Sure, that's part of having a conversation."

"Why are you here? I mean, you're lovely and fabulous. What could you want with me? I'm three months pregnant and my last ex was a psycho. I'm pretty sure I'm damaged."

"Oh, honey, we're all damaged in some way. Now, eat your food so I can take you out for ice cream. "

"Ice cream?"

"Sure. You didn't think the date would stop at dinner, did you?"

"But you haven't answered my question."

"Does there have to be a reason?"

"I'd like one, yes."

"How about because something about you has bewitched me and I want the chance to return the favour?"

Poppy swallowed thickly and her cheeks bloomed red again. Yep, there was that spark again. "That's good." Poppy said. "That's lovely."

"Good, we're agreed! Now eat some more of your dinner! Ice cream awaits!"

Chapter Sixty

"Do you think I should let Mike and William know what's going on?" Blaine asked.

Justin nodded. "That would be a good idea. Chuck too, if you can track him down. And let your grandmother know, too. She'll want to know."

They sat in the waiting room of the emergency room. Blaine was at a loss for what to say, for what to do. He had never seen Nancy looking so distraught, so filled with rage. Normally, nothing in life phased Nancy, but he was rattled by this. Hell, they all were.

He pulled out his phone and had just finished sending texts to Mike and Chuck when Rebecca came into the waiting room. She carried four coffees in a tray.

"It tastes like shit, but it'll do the job," she said, handing each of them a cup. "The other one is for Nancy, but I don't think he's in any fit state to drink anything at the moment. He's only got eyes for Devon."

"It's kind of sad they had to come together this way, though," Blaine said.

"Hey, Devon deserved what he got."

Her words shocked him. "What do you mean?"

Rebecca huffed out a breath. "That sounded mean. But it's true. I mean, when he first told me that he loved Nancy, I said that was great, he could give up hooking! But he chose to do it for the money and walked away from love."

"Sometimes people need to have the rug pulled out from under them, to have their world shaken up, before they see sense. I know what you mean," Justin said.

"I still think it's a horrible thing to say," Blaine crossed his arms and ignored his coffee. "So what? He deserved this? No one deserves this."

"I talked to Devon about quitting hooking all the time! You know there are lots of nasty fags out there, that men have died. He could have been one of them." She placed a hand on Blaine's knee. "I'm sorry. That was insensitive of me. I was always just so fucking worried about him."

When tears sprang to her eyes, making the green of them look somehow more luminescent, Blaine calmed down. "I'm sorry, too. Your heart was in the right place."

"How long have you known Devon?" Justin asked.

"God, for ages. He was my last boyfriend before I came out of the closet, then he came out shortly thereafter. Apparently my courage to be who I really was inspired him to do the same."

"How long ago was that?" Blaine asked.

"High school. We've known each other for a long time."

"When did he start hooking?"

"A long time. Nearly ten years by this point. I've begged him to stop, to find another job that paid well. Told him again and again that he didn't have to always have the best of everything, that no one cared about his image. He wouldn't listen though, and now look what's happened." More tears came to her eyes. "God, he could have died! He could have been killed and I would have lost my best friend."

They let her cry it out. Blaine hugged her from one side and Justin put his arms around her on the other side. They sat there like that for a few minutes, whether grieving what could have been or feeling remorse for what had happened, it didn't matter. Sometimes you just needed that moment of physical contact to bring comfort.

There was the sound of footsteps. Blaine looked up and

saw Nancy standing there. His face was a mess of tears and his eyes were red from crying.

"He's awake again."

That was all he said before turning to go back into the hospital room. Blaine, Justin, and Rebecca followed.

Chapter Sixty-One

Nancy was already at Devon's side when they entered.

He held one of Devon's hands. To Blaine, it looked almost unnatural, seeing that unblemished hand surrounded by a mountain of bandages with blood soaking into them. Devon held up his other hand and waved weakly. "Hi. Where's the party?"

Blaine walked up to the bed and Justin stayed with Rebecca. "Devon, do you remember who did this?"

"Yeah, his name was David. Long blond hair, blue eyes that were so deep it was like they were looking into you. Messed up dude; angry man." He coughed and, despite the situation, Blaine was touched to see Nancy hold out a cup of water with a straw so that Devon could take a drink. When he was done, Devon looked at him with what Blaine knew was love in his eyes. Blaine knew that was exactly the look he wore when he looked at Justin.

Even though his worst suspicions had been confirmed, Blaine wasn't angry. He was a little ashamed of himself for being thankful that it hadn't been him. It could have been him, all too easily. David could have beaten him to a pulp, but all he did was to whittle away at Blaine's self-worth. He didn't know what was worse.

"What do you want to do now, Devon?" Justin asked this, trying to keep his voice light.

"He's going to charge the fucker," Nancy said.

"Damn right he is!" Rebecca said.

"No. I'm not," Devon said.

Nancy looked at him, shocked. "What do you mean? He could have killed you!"

"Yes, which is why I'm lucky. He could have killed me, but didn't."

"But why don't you want to charge him?" Nancy said. "He has to pay for what he's done!"

"And he will. Honestly, I was lucky I got home, lucky I was able to find my way back."

"How did you get home? What happened after David... did this?" Justin asked.

"I just remember waking up in the back of David's car. He drove me back to my place and got me inside."

"Why would he do that?" Blaine asked.

"I don't know. He carried me up to my apartment and left me there. I was bleeding all over my bed and he left me there."

"Did he say anything?" Justin asked.

"Only that I got what I deserved and that he forgave me."

The words echoed what David had said to him and Blaine shivered. Something still didn't make sense though. David would more than likely have just chucked Devon in an alleyway. It made more sense to Blaine that Devon would have had David over to his place. He didn't think Devon was being entirely truthful about what had happened, and he didn't know why.

It wasn't his place to say anything though. What Devon needed now was time to heal. And Nancy; he clearly needed Nancy. What had happened was horrible, but it seemed to put a few things into perspective for Devon, and for that, Blaine was thankful.

"We'll leave you alone now. You let us know if you need anything." He turned to Nancy. "You coming, Nancy?"

"I'm going to stay here for a bit longer, if that's okay."

Blaine thought that Nancy would sleep at the hospital if he was allowed to. "Okay, but not too long, all right?"

Rebecca kissed Devon on the forehead before leaving and promising to visit the next day. She came out into the hallway and joined Blaine and Justin. "God, I need a drink," she said.

Blaine thought of Nan and her spiked pink lemonade. "I know just the place. You can come with us."

"Thank God," She huffed out another breath. They walked down the hallway towards the exit. "I just can't figure it out. None of it makes sense. Why was Devon lying to us?"

"I've been asking myself the same question," Blaine replied.

Chapter Sixty-Two

The ice cream shop was filled with people, even at this late hour. Poppy couldn't believe that people ate ice cream at this time of night, but then she was there too, right?

Poppy still wondered what in the hell she was doing, but she didn't care. It was wonderful to be out and about with a woman she was attracted to. Nothing else mattered except relaxing into the moment.

She had spent so much of her life fighting against everything she wanted to do, everything she knew, everything she held dear. Well, that stopped now. Right now, all Poppy wanted to do was get to know more about this woman that struck something within her.

They ordered their ice cream, each getting a vanilla swirl cone. They sat outside where the sounds of traffic were a musical backdrop against the conversations going on around them. They ate their ice cream in silence for a bit, just enjoying the moment. For Poppy's part, she was amazed at how comfortable she was with Dava already.

There were things she wanted to know, however, so she broke the silence. "Can I ask you something?"

Dava gave her a wink. "You can ask me anything you want to."

"Well, I mean, you know I'm pregnant, right? So why would you want to get involved in any way, shape, or form with me? I mean, I'm going to have a baby, for Christ's sake."

"So?" Dava replied. "It doesn't make you any less attractive. It doesn't make you any less of a woman."

"But I'm going to push something the size of a melon out of my twat. That's so not a turn on."

"Oh, but it is. You could have chosen to get rid of the baby. Hell, most normal women would."

"Great, so I'm abnormal."

"That's not a bad thing. I hate normal people, so boring. And I meant that there are thousands of women who opt to get rid of the baby, lesbian or not. You chose to keep it, and that says something about you and about the strength of your character."

Touched, all Poppy could do was try not to cry. "Thank you," she said.

Dava smiled. "No need to get all weepy on me, it's the truth. Hell, a lot of women would have caved in the relationship you were in and just lived inside it. Though, you can't really call a relationship like that living."

"Oh, Connie wasn't abusive. She never hit me."

"She didn't have to. She was abusive to herself. An angry person like that, well, they're poison. It took guts to kick her ass out the door. Have you thought of any names yet?"

The abrupt switch in topic covered Poppy off guard, but she answered. "If it's a boy, I was thinking of naming him after Blaine. If it's a girl, I was thinking of naming it after my mom."

"What's your mother's name?"

"Her name was Emily. She passed away when I was a girl."

Dava put down her ice cream cone and took both of Poppy's hands in hers. "I know that she'd be very proud of you."

"I'd like to hope so."

"I know so. I'm proud of you."

"You barely know me."

"But what I know, I like. Quite a lot."

Poppy blushed, but let the word she wanted to say, and normally would have held back, slip past her lips. "And I like you."

Poppy wasn't aware of their faces coming closer, or who had started kissing whom. All she knew was that one moment she was staring into Dava's eyes and the next, she was kissing her. Dava tasted of smoke and ice cream. Poppy had never tasted anything so wonderful.

Chapter Sixty-Three

Mike was worried. He was worried about Nancy and distraught over Devon. More so, he was very worried that Chuck would go and do something stupid over Sebastian. How had things gotten so fucked up so quickly?

They had stayed at The Cabin. William had gone to the bar and brought them back shots of whiskey. Mike had shaken his head. "I'm not in the mood to drink."

"I know, but you need this for courage."

"Then why do you have one?"

William sighed. "Okay, I need this and I don't want to drink alone."

That had gotten a smile out of Mike. They had followed the shot with a few beers, and then followed those with a couple of screwdrivers. Mike told himself the entire time that he was drinking because he was worried about his friends, but then why did being worried feel so fun at the moment?

Mike saw the worried look on his face. "Michael, it's okay. It is. Justin and Blaine are with Nancy, and Chuck's a big boy, he can take care of himself. He's done it for years, hasn't he? And Nancy and Devon will be fine."

"It didn't sound like Devon was fine. He wouldn't be if he ended up in the hospital."

"You worry too much. They're big boys, Michael. They've been through this before."

"No one we've known has ever been beaten to a pulp before by someone we used to know."

"We didn't really know David. He was Blaine's man, and he didn't get close to us, really."

"We still knew him. We had him over in the beginning,

don't you remember?"

"Course I do. I let him suck me off in the bathroom and then when he went to take his out, he had the smallest dick I'd ever seen. I laughed at him and told him that would be a waste of my time."

"You never told me that!"

"We had a play and don't tell rule, remember? So I played and didn't tell you. Didn't think anything of it at the time."

Mike was horrified by his casual tone. "Why are you being like this?"

"And why are you being a pussy?"

Mike took a good look at William then and saw what he should have seen before: William was pissed drunk. While he'd always been able to hold his liquor, William had always been a lightweight. Mike told himself that William's words were brought on by drink and nothing more.

"You've had enough. I'm driving us home. Give me the keys."

"We'll leave when I'm good and ready. God, when did you turn into such a woman? I'm going to take a piss." He stomped off to the bathroom, leaving Mike alone.

Letting out an annoyed breath, Mike texted Blaine and Justin to see if there were any updates. He got a response back from Blaine almost instantly: *Lots. We're heading to Nan's. Meet us there?*

Mike texted back: Give me thirty minutes.

Then he went in search of William. He went into the washroom but didn't see him right away. He looked around and still didn't see him, but then he heard the voices coming from a toilet stall.

"Harder." William's voice. "Suck, don't blow, I don't have all night."

There was a sound like something being unstuck. "It's not my fault you're not getting hard."

Mike stood there rooted to the spot. He was frozen and wondered if he'd ever be warm again. Steeling himself for what he was about to see, he strode forward and knocked on the door to the handicapped stall, the only one big enough to hold two people comfortably.

"William." That was all he said. That was all he could say.

"Shit man, who's that?" This was the other man, whispering as if Mike couldn't hear him.

Mike pounded one the door and began pulling at it, the words erupting out of his mouth in a rage. "I'm his fucking husband, you piece of shit! Now open the fucking door before I break it the fuck in!"

The latch turned and the door opened. Mike saw a regular at the bar on his knees in front of William, his cock out and rock hard. William's dick was out too, but it was far from up. It hung like a sad, deflated windsock. On the back of the toilet were a brown vial, powder, and a small silver spoon.

William stood there looking like a sad puppy. He actually held out his arms to him beseechingly. "Michael." There was pain and regret in that voice.

Mike didn't say anything. There was nothing to say, really.

Instead, Mike turned his back on William and walked out of the bathroom and out of the bar, leaving a piece of his heart behind him with each step. Mike had an overly romantic notion of William following the trail of his broken heart, like Hansel and Gretel, but he didn't think that very likely. When he was at the car, he made sure to keep the last piece of his heart for himself.

Then he got in and drove away.

Chapter Sixty-Four

Nan was helping herself to some pink lemonade. She made it for the kids all the time and it brought them comfort. Now she was the one that needed comforting.

She had no idea what to do. She had made a mess of things, she knew that. Nan also knew that it was time to tell Blaine the truth, that he had a right to know everything. She just wished that telling him was an easy thing to do.

Nan knew that if she told him the truth (not if, when), it would damage things between them. He would eventually have to be told that he was working with his father and that she was his mother, thus tearing away thirty three years' worth of lies.

She hadn't meant to lie to him, hadn't thought of doing it at first. She had meant to raise him to be proud of who he was, no matter how he turned out. How could she have started lying to him because she was so ashamed of herself?

The idea that Poppy would tell Blaine her secret should have kept her awake at night, but it wasn't even that. What kept her awake was the fact that she had lied to the person who meant the most to her. She lived the lie and went to great lengths to hide the truth about herself.

It pained her to know they had never achieved the bond of mother and son. They could have a much deeper relationship than they had now, if only she had told him the truth. She no longer trusted her own motives for lying. She should have been proud of what had happened with Ernest, not ashamed. They had created something so wonderful and she had hidden behind lies instead.

Nan was pouring vodka into her lemonade when the door

opened. Nan was surprised to see Blaine and Justin come through the door with a lady that she didn't know. Blaine looked sheepish. "I hope you don't mind us just dropping in on you, Nan."

"Don't be silly dear, you're always welcome. I was just about to pour myself a drink. Would the three of you care for something to wet your whistles?"

"That would be great." Blaine hugged her, pulling her to him in a hard embrace. "It's been one hell of a night."

"Why don't you introduce me to your friend and I'll get the drinks ready?"

As Nan poured more pink lemonade and vodka into glasses, Justin and Blaine talked. They introduced her to Rebecca and told her what had happened.

She listened with shock and growing horror. Finally, she could hold back her words no longer. "That David is an evil, terrible boy." She huffed out a breath. "There, I've said it." Turning to Blaine, Nan sighed. "I never liked him or how he treated you. You're worth so much more than that."

Blaine smiled and took Justin's left hand in his own. "I know. I know that now."

"I'm sorry, I'm speaking out of turn. He just got my garters in such a fucking twist."

"You have garters, Nan? That's kind of hot," Blaine said.

Nan almost spit out the sip of juice and vodka she had taken. "You're a dirty boy! What would your mother say?"

"I don't know. What would you say?"

Nan's heart stopped in her chest. She could actually feel all the colour seeping from her face. "What did you say?"

"I said, what would you say?"

"I... I'm not your mother."

"Yes, you are. Poppy told me."

Chapter Sixty-Five

Nan was speechless for a moment.

She wanted to rush over and put her arms around Blaine, letting him know how sorry she was. Instead, she remained where she was and just let her words pour out. "Blaine, I'm sorry. She wasn't supposed to say anything!"

"I'm glad she did. It confirmed what I've suspected for a long time."

Justin looked at Rebecca. "Maybe we should give them some alone time."

"It's okay," Nan said. "He'll tell you afterwards anyways." She looked back at Blaine. "I'm sorry. So sorry."

"Don't be. I don't hold anything against you. I knew that you'd tell me in your own time. It's a big secret to carry around, it would take time to reveal it."

"But I didn't get a chance to tell you in my own way! When did Poppy tell you?"

"Right after she left here. She called me."

"Typical, she has always had a big mouth," Nan said waspishly. She took a sip of her vodka-infused lemonade and then took another. "What must you think of me?"

Blaine put his drink down and came over to her, taking her own glass and putting it down beside his. Then he took her hands in his own and looked her right in the eyes. "I think you're still the woman that raised me, the woman that loved me when I had no one else. You are my rock and my safety net. You taught me how to be a good boy and I was able to grow into a good man because of you."

He gave her a quizzical look and she wondered whether he'd speak further. When he did, it was strained slightly. "I do have two questions though. The first is, why didn't you tell me? I would have been proud to have you as my mother."

"Oh, Blainey, I was so ashamed. I was about to marry the man that I thought I'd be with for the rest of my life. When he left me, I was pregnant with you. It was all rolled up into that rage and anger. I felt I was too old to be a mother. I looked at all the other mothers, young, not a day over forty. And there I was, over forty, my chance at happiness gone. You were all I had left in the world and I didn't want to embarrass you, this old crone as your mother. It was selfish, I know that now. You had a right to know and I shouldn't have kept it from you."

"I understand why you did. I don't hold it against you. But the second question is: who is my father?"

Nan was caught short. "You mean, Poppy didn't tell you?"

He shook his head. "She said that was far more complicated and you had to tell me that part."

"I can't believe she told you that I was your mother but didn't tell you who your father was."

"Poppy said that some secrets are best revealed by the parties involved. So who is he?"

"You already know him. I'll let him tell you though. Hold on a second, I have to go make a phone call, see if he can come over." She left the room.

They were silent for a moment. Rebecca was the first to speak. "So your grandmother is really your mother?"

"Yep."

Justin looked at Blaine with a slightly pained expression. "Why didn't you tell me?"

"I was mad at first and had to work through it in my own time. I was going to tell you, but we were here and the moment seemed right. I'm sorry, I didn't mean to keep anything from you."

"With all due respect," Rebecca said, "we've had a lot going on. It's a lot to take in. I would have done the same thing. Not that it's any of my business but it's just my opinion."

"It's okay, babe. I would have lost it but you're handling it a lot better than I would have," Justin said. He leaned forward and kissed him softly on the lips. "Who do you think your father is?"

"I don't know. But if that secret is anything like the one that Nan was carrying, anything is possible." He took a sip of his lemonade. "With my luck, it's probably a drag queen!"

They all waited a moment and then Justin, Rebecca, and Blaine all started laughing. Nan walked into the room and looked at them.

"Guess I put too much vodka in the lemonade. Youth, no alcohol tolerance at all!"

Chapter Sixty-Six

Nancy sat beside Devon's hospital bed and thought.

Though Nancy was a very grounded individual, he had a sixth sense about things. He'd actually written about physic phenomena for different magazines, along with poetry and short stories. He was toying with the idea for a novel. However, you didn't need to be a physic to know that Devon was full of shit.

Something about what he had said didn't ring true. It all sounded so flimsy. Nancy didn't want to poke and prod, but he had a right to know what was really going on. So he poked and prodded Devon until he woke up.

Devon regarded Nancy with sleepy eyes and when he smiled at him, Nancy's nerve almost crumbled. How could he demand to know something when Devon was in so much pain? However, Nancy knew that he wouldn't sleep until he learned the truth.

"Hey, handsome," Devon said. His voice was so soft he was almost whispering.

"Hey, yourself." Nancy reached out and took one of Devon's hands. "Listen. You know you can talk straight with me, right?"

"Of course I do."

"Then do you want to tell me what really happened today?"

Devon's smile widened. "I did tell you what happened."

"No, you didn't. Not everything."

"I did."

"No, you didn't. There are holes in your story big enough to drive a truck through."

"I don't know what you're talking about."

Nancy reminded himself to stay calm, to talk to Devon with a soothing voice. It was hard though. "Devon, you know I love you. But a man like David doesn't do what he did and drive you home for no reason. I'd like to help you, but I have to know what you're not telling me. Can't you be honest with me for once?"

"I have been honest with you."

"You're not being honest with me now. Just tell me what happened."

"You're not going to let this go, are you?"

"No, I'm not."

Devon sighed. The sound was one of defeat and resignation. Nancy was impressed that Devon was able to communicate that without saying a word. If he wasn't concentrating so much on remaining calm, he would have told him so.

Finally, Devon looked at him again. "What I told you up until the moment I passed out was true. All of it. David beat me more out of frustration because he couldn't get it up than anything."

"Okay."

"He didn't just drive me home though. When I woke up, he was standing over me. He had finally got his cock hard and he was stroking it. He said he'd only take me home if I gave him a blowjob. He offered me three hundred dollars to do it. I usually only get twenty dollars for a blow-job. I think he felt guilty for what he'd done."

"I should damn well hope so, the fucker!" Nancy forgot about remaining calm. "I hope you told him he could be happy with Sally Handsome and her five finger sisters!"

Devon didn't say anything.

"Tell me you didn't. Please tell me you didn't give that fucker a blowjob after what he had done to you."

Devon still didn't say anything for a minute or two. When he spoke, his voice was filled with regret. "I'm sorry, Clarence. I needed some way to get home and I needed the money. It didn't mean anything, truly it didn't."

"You should have called the police! You should have called an ambulance! You shouldn't have let Rebecca find you in a bloody heap in your apartment!"

"Clarence, I'm sorry." Devon reached out for Nancy's hand but Nancy pulled his hand away.

"So am I," he said.

Gathering up his coat and bag, Nancy walked out of the hospital room, fighting the temptation to look back with every step.

Chapter Sixty-Seven

Sebastian was trying to soothe his heart when he heard the yelling outside his window.

After Chuck had left, Sebastian poured himself some more wine and finished half a glass. The wine wasn't doing anything to numb the pain in his chest, however. It was as if Chuck had reached into him and pulled his heart out. He had never felt such pain. Then again, he had never been in love with anyone before.

Sure, there had been a few guys he had dated when he was younger, but he was never into them as he had been into Chuck. Being a girl was tough, especially if you knew you weren't one. After his gender reassignment surgery, he'd dated a few men, but always stopped short of the big reveal. Sure, he'd sucked his fair share of cocks, but that was it. Chuck was the first guy he wanted to sleep with, the first man Sebastian wanted to be completely honest with.

So when Chuck not only walked out but ran as fast as he could away from him, Sebastian was crushed. He felt dirty, as if there was a mark on his skin that he couldn't get off, no matter how hard he washed.

Instead of taking a shower to feel clean again, Sebastian drank. He wasn't one to overindulge in booze but hey, there was a first time for everything. Putting the wine down, Sebastian poured himself a healthy dose of whiskey. When he washed that down, Sebastian poured himself another helping.

He took the glass to the living room and sat there in the half dark, wondering if he had done the right thing. If he had been right to trust Chuck with his deepest secret. He thought he had been. Then again, love does strange things to people, warps their vision. They didn't call it love blindness for nothing.

What surprised Sebastian was how quick he had fallen for Chuck. Perhaps he'd loved him since that first kiss in the bathhouse. When he had seen Chuck ride on the pink horse, had ridden behind him, and heard his laughter, that love nearly made his heart shoot out of his chest.

He was about to go back to the kitchen to pour himself another glass of whiskey when he heard the yelling. He went to his living room window and looked out. Chuck was underneath his balcony and was yelling something unintelligible through the glass. He opened up his balcony door and the words became clear.

"Sebastian! Sebastian! Hey, Sebastian!"

The pain in Chuck's voice was real. Sebastian wanted to remain cold, wanted to stay chilled and angry and hurt, but hearing the pain in Chuck's voice hurt him even more.

Walking to the edge of his balcony, Sebastian stepped into the light. "I hear you loud and clear, turkey. In fact, so do all my neighbours."

Chuck looked up at him, his face bathed in light and shadow. Chuck saw that his eyes were rimmed red and he had been crying. He looked dreadful. "Sebastian, oh thank God, thank God, please let me come up, please! I'm so sorry, so sorry, you don't know how sorry I am!"

"I'm beginning to have some idea. Are you drunk?"

"I had to have a few drinks to get up the courage to come back here! I wasn't sure you'd want to see me, wasn't sure what you'd do."

"Well, screaming my name under my balcony is a good way to get my attention."

"Please let me come up, please. I was wrong, you're all

man, you're a total man, you're the man for me and I want you so much. Please."

For his part, Sebastian thought about resisting, turning him away, telling Chuck to go home and never bother him again, but Sebastian realized his heart already belonged to Chuck.

"Come around front. I'll buzz you in."

Chapter Sixty-Eight

When the buzzer went off less than a minute later, Sebastian wondered if Chuck had run the entire way around the building. Deciding to play with Chuck a little, he pressed the buzzer and spoke into the voice box. "Yes?"

"Sebastian. It's me."

"I don't know anyone named 'me.' You'll have to be a little bit more specific than that. You could be anyone."

"It's Chuck, Sebastian; we were just talking outside your window. When you looked down at me, I could see the pale green of your eyes and they looked like sapphires in the darkness."

A laugh escaped Sebastian's mouth despite himself. "You mean emeralds, don't you? Sapphires are blue."

"Emeralds, that's what I said."

"Come on up, turkey."

Pressing the buzzer, Sebastian disconnected and waited, wondering if he was making a mistake. He loved Chuck, God knew he did. There were a few problems, though. Did he want to date a guy that went to the bathhouse on a regular basis? Chuck clearly had commitment issues; did he want to deal with any of those? And was he the jealous type? He didn't really know anything about him, really, only that his heart and his body wanted him.

There was a knock at his apartment door. Opening it slowly revealed Chuck, who was panting heavily. There were tears in his eyes. Despite himself, Sebastian was moved to see him so emotional, even if he was clearly drunk.

"Can I come in?" Chuck said softly.

"Why else would I have answered the door?"

Stepping back from the door to let Chuck pass by him, Sebastian tried not to be turned on by Chuck, by how he smelled, how he looked. He even remembered how Chuck tasted and found himself getting hard. "Down boy," he whispered.

"I didn't do anything. Yet," Chuck said.

"I wasn't talking to you."

"Will you, though? Or, will you let me talk to you?"

"How much have you had to drink?"

"Well, I had a drink or two with the guys. Then a few drinks before I went to the bathhouse."

"You went to a bathhouse?"

"I couldn't do anything, don't you see? It all makes sense now, what I'm feeling for you, what I need from you."

"You lost me and I'm still stuck at the part where you went to a bathhouse."

Chuck let out a rough breath and ran his hands through his hair. "I'm making a mess of things, aren't I?"

"No, you already have. But you're still fucking cute."

"Oh, that's a relief. Can I start again?"

"Let me get some liquid refreshment first."

Heading into the kitchen, Sebastian poured himself another half glass of whiskey and poured one for Chuck, too, not that he needed it, apparently. However, it wasn't good to drink alone. Passing the extra glass to Chuck, Sebastian took a sip of his own drink and let the liquid warm first his throat and then his stomach. He looked at Chuck again and said, "Now, you may start over. But it had better be good. I'm still deciding whether or not to forgive you."

Chapter Sixty-Nine

Chuck's heart was in his throat.

He wasn't sure if that was because he was half drunk or if he was afraid. He was terrified of losing Sebastian. He was afraid of losing the best thing that had ever happened to him.

"I understand," Chuck said. "Running out of here was a cowardly thing to do."

"Yes. It was."

"But you have to understand. I've never done this before."

"What? Never been with a guy who was a girl?"

"I've never been in love before."

Sebastian was shocked. "Never? You've never loved anyone before?"

"No, not really. I was in lust a lot, I thought I loved other guys, but it was easier to just fuck 'em and move on. My father brought me up believing in the Four F's."

"I don't think I've heard that one."

"Find them, feel them, fuck them, and then forget them. He had a string of marriages and ended up alone. He told me not to end up like him in the end, to find love. The only problem was that I didn't know how to. Not until you."

Sebastian swallowed thickly. "So, why did you leave? Because I used to be a woman? Because you couldn't handle the truth?"

"No. That was just an excuse. The truth was I was afraid of how much I loved you. I was afraid of how much you filled my thoughts, my heart. I was just afraid. You are the only man that I could ever see spending the rest of my life with and that frightened the fuck out of me."

"The rest of your life?" Sebastian choked the words out.

Chuck saw that Sebastian was crying but Chuck continued anyway, despite how afraid he was. He had already begun and couldn't stop now. He had to get the words out.

"The rest of my life. I don't care that you were a woman, I don't give a shit. I look at you and I only see you, the beautiful man that I fell in love with and love more than anything I've loved before. And I'm so afraid that I'm going to fuck things up."

"You kind of already did."

"Don't say that. We can work past this, we can. God, all I can think of is you; all I want to do is love you and make love to you."

"There's still the matter of you going to the bathhouse," Sebastian said softly. "You still haven't told me about that."

"God, I'm sorry. I don't know why I went, maybe just to tell myself that I was over you, that you didn't mean anything."

"So what happened?"

"I went in there and all I could think of was you. There were all sorts of guys there, but none of them held a candle to you. I couldn't do anything except run to you and beg you to forgive me. I know I don't deserve your forgiveness, but I had to come, I had to see you, had to ask. I had to tell you how I felt."

Chuck took a deep breath and finished the rest of his whiskey in one shot. He pulled his shoulders up and sighed. "I guess that's it then. I'll leave you alone."

"What do you mean?"

"I'll go. I know you don't want me around. I've ruined things, I know that. I've lost you and I deserve that. I'll be going now."

Chuck shuffled towards the door until Sebastian's voice

spoke out behind him. "Where are you going, turkey?"

Turning around, Chuck looked at Sebastian. "What do you mean?"

"I mean, where are you going? Did I tell you to leave?"

"No."

"Then why are you going?"

"Because you haven't said anything. I figured we were done."

"God, you're such a drama queen. I didn't say anything because I was moved. Because you made me speechless. And you made me realize how much I'm in love with you."

A sob escaped Chuck's throat and then he ran across the living room and threw himself into Sebastian's arms. Then he was kissing him and kissing him some more, his heart beating quickly with love for him, and he lost himself in the touch of the man he loved more than anything in the world.

"Would you like to spend the night?"

"God, yes."

"Then let me take you to bed."

As Sebastian took his hand and led him towards the bedroom, he wondered how his body could possibly be big enough to hold his heart.

Chapter Seventy

Nancy sat alone in the dark.

He guessed he should have seen this all coming, that his gut feeling about Devon was right all along. Why did he always choose the unobtainable man? Why did he always fall in love with the guy he couldn't have?

Nancy knew he was worth more than some guy who preferred hooking instead of being with him, but he hoped, God he hoped, that Devon would realize how special he was and give up hooking. He knew he had been fooling himself, that he was silly to have given his heart to Devon, that it had been foolish of him. He was so desperate for love that he was willing to love anyone.

He just wished that taking his heart back didn't hurt so much.

Why did something that was made to fuel your body feel so many different emotions? Studies had shown that the heart was merely a muscle, that its job was mainly to keep things running, that its purpose was to help the body function. There were even studies that showed it was impossible for the heart to feel love.

Then why did the heart mourn? Why did it hurt? Why did it grieve? Nancy knew it was more than the spirit doing these things; it was the heart, too. If it didn't feel emotion, why did his feel like it was bleeding?

He did something he hadn't done in a long time. He opened up his computer and clicked open a word document. Then he began to write.

Nancy wasn't sure what it was about writing that was so soothing to him, but it was his happy place. He didn't share any of his writing with anyone else. He made his money on graphic design, on websites and promotional materials. His writing was just for him.

It brought him comfort like nothing else could. He liked to lose himself in the words, in the cadence and characters. When he wrote, it was as if the world and everything in it disappeared; all that existed were his words.

He was typing away on his keyboard when his phone rang. He was distracted by what he was writing so he didn't look at his call display. He answered with a quick "Hello?"

"Nancy, thank goodness you picked up."

Nancy's blood froze. "Devon, why are you calling me?"

"Nancy, you have to listen to me."

"Oh honey, I've done all the listening to you I'm going to do."

"Look, I didn't mean for anything to happen."

"Oh, so you didn't mean to go over to David's to suck his dick and get paid for it? You had no intention of doing that? That's a real comfort, I'm glad we've cleared up that misunderstanding."

"Nancy, don't be like that, you know I love you."

"Oh honey, that's rich coming from you. I don't think you know what love is. I truly don't."

"I do and I know I love you."

"You have some piss poor way of showing it. Standing me up to go have sex, blowing me off to blow some other guy, hooking up with the abusive ex of my best friend for money so you could pay your rent. Yeah, that's love all right, I'm absolutely smitten."

"Nancy, look, if you'd only listen –"

"I have listened, and I've tried to hear your side of things, tried to understand. But the truth is I deserve more than you're

197

willing to give me, more than you could ever give. You're a selfish, miserable fuck and I hope you find what you're looking for, but it's not me. I'm worth more than you."

He hung up the phone, tears stinging his eyes. He hated that he was crying over Devon, hated that he had reduced him to tears again, but he felt that crying was part of letting go, so he let the tears come as they wanted. It would only hurt to hold them back.

His phone rang again, and Nancy stabbed at the 'accept call button'. "Look, I told you, you fucking asshole, we're done, get it? We're motherfucking done."

"Gee, if that's how you really feel about me, I guess that's it then," Mike said.

"Mike? God, I'm sorry, I thought you were Devon."

"What did he do now?"

"Long story. What's up, honey? You okay?"

"No, not really. I don't know what I am anymore."

"Don't be silly. You're you, Michael the Fabulous, Michael the Awesome. What's wrong?"

"I could really use a friend right now."

"Couldn't we all. Did you want to talk about it?"

"Do you mind? I don't want to keep you from anything."

"Just writing. Friends are more important. Give me five minutes to get ready and I'll meet you at Ada's. I've had enough of bars for a while."

"Okay, I'll see you in a bit."

Nancy hung up and was just about to go and throw on some fresh body glitter when his phone rang again. He looked at the call display this time and saw Blaine's number. "Blaine honey, what is it?"

"Can you come over to Nan's? I'm about to find out who my father is! I want you here when I meet him."

"Oh honey! Give me ten minutes! I'll go pick up Mikey on the way over. We'll be there soon; I don't want to miss this moment!"

Nancy hung up the phone, wondering about fate. He supposed that some things just worked out the way they were supposed to. It was the way of life.

Nancy just wished he could figure his life out. Oh well, he would live vicariously through others for now. He hoped Nan had some pink lemonade made. He gave himself one last look in the mirror.

A lady had to look great for her public, after all.

Chapter Seventy-One

Blaine was on the edge of his seat.

He had imagined his father countless times over the years as an army hero, as a jet fighter, as a secret spy. When he was older, he thought his father might be the kind of guy who would do volunteer work for the UN or work overseas. Anything that would account for him not being there.

To think that finally, after all this time, he would get to meet his father... well, he just couldn't contain himself. Justin put a hand on his shoulder. "Babe, you're going to wear a hole in the floor."

Blaine realized that he had been pacing, too excited to stay still. Rebecca gave him a small smile. "For what it's worth, I'd be nervous too."

"That's some small comfort."

"Well, think about it. You're about to meet someone who hasn't been part of your life and welcome them with open arms. I know, I had to do that with my mom."

"What happened with her?" Justin asked.

"I was adopted by my parents. They've been great, don't get me wrong, but you always wonder, right?" She took a sip of her lemonade. "My mom found me three years ago, tracked me down."

"You didn't track her down?" Blaine asked.

"Oh, I wanted to, I really did, but didn't know where to begin. Then I got this call from a woman I didn't know and when she told me who she was, I almost hit the roof. I had all sorts of emotions running through me, all sort of thoughts. In the end, I tried to hold it together until I met her, then I would let fate decide."

"So what happened?" Blaine asked.

"We're best friends. My adoptive parents get along really well with her, and she's like a sister to me. It doesn't always happen, but I was lucky. My mother runs an inn about an hour from here. I go and see her there often, and we go on shopping trips. It's kind of nice." She took another sip and put her glass down, coming towards Blaine. "Point is, just be kind to him, he'll have had his own reasons for doing what he did."

Blaine gave Rebecca a hug. She had become such a good friend in such a short amount of time. "Thank you."

"Don't mention it. It is what it is, right? Just remember to breathe and maybe ease up a little on the booze."

Turning to look at the half empty bottle of vodka, Blaine could only laugh. "It has been a boozer of an evening, hasn't it?"

Nan came back into the room, wringing her hands. "Blaine honey, there's something I should tell you before your father arrives."

"It's okay, Mom."

Nan stopped short. "You've never called me that before." Tears had sprung to her eyes.

"It's okay. I'll stop if you want me to."

"Don't be silly; it was wonderful." She wiped at her eyes. "The thing is, before your father shows up, you should know something about him."

"Mom, I said it's okay. It doesn't matter who he is, just as long as he has a reason for leaving both of us. I'll be kind to him, I promise."

The front door opened and Blaine was shocked to see Romilda Robinson enter his mother's house. He was even more shocked when Romilda came towards him and embraced him.

"My son," she said, "I'm so happy to really meet you. Officially, that is, and not in the library!" She gave a hearty chuckle and only then noticed how silent the kitchen had become.

Chapter Seventy-Two

"Was it something I said?" Romilda asked.

She looked around the room and took in everyone's shocked faces. She sighed. It was something she was used to, living in a world that seemed to view her as a second-class citizen just because she was born in the wrong gender.

Only Cordelia looked happy to see her. She came towards her and put a comforting hand on her arm. "Blaine? I'd like you to meet your father," she said quietly.

Romilda braced herself. She was prepared for the worst. Blaine would react one of two ways: either with horror, or with amazement and disdain. She had seen it all before, was used to people's dramatic reactions. What she wasn't prepared for was his laughter.

There was nothing derisive in it, though. There was only humour. Blaine laughed until tears were running down his face and he had to bend over to catch his breath. He looked up with a big, bright smile and just screamed the words "Drag Queen!" before losing himself in another fit of giggles.

Romilda looked at Cordelia and was pleased to see that she looked just as confused. "Cordy, I'd have that boy looked at if I were you. He's not quite right in the head."

Blaine shook his head trying to quiet his laughter. While he was gathering himself together, Justin spoke. "He's just laughing at the irony of it all."

"Irony? I'm ironic?"

"No, you're not, but he made a crack before you came over, that with his luck, his father would end up being a drag queen."

"Is that what you were all laughing about earlier?" Nan asked, letting out a little chuckle. "Well, I do have to admit, that is pretty funny."

Bristling, Romilda fixed Cordelia with a hard stare. "I'm much more than a drag queen, thank you. I'm a woman through and through, not some cheap man playing parlour tricks for pennies."

"He didn't mean any offense, it's just ironic, that's all," Cordelia said.

"When you all stop trying to decide what's ironic, then maybe we can have a real conversation."

"Oh, Ms. Robinson," Justin said. "Calm down, you just weren't here for that conversation. We're all a little shocked, to be honest."

Those words calmed her. Letting out a sigh, Romilda smiled. "I'm sorry, dear boy, just on edge is all. I never thought you'd really know who I was to you, Blaine. I didn't think anyone would know."

Blaine had quieted down and was looking at her with deep brown eyes. "How do you feel?"

"Honestly? Relieved. I was so tired of pretending, so tired of the charade. It's been an up and down road for me and I'm quite happy to have reached a plateau, truth be told."

"Why didn't you tell me?" Blaine asked softly.

"My dear boy, Cordelia had me under such a tight lock and key that I had no choice but to be in your life from afar or as your boss at the library."

"Didn't you care about me at all? Didn't you want to tell me who you were?"

"Every time I saw you. Every time I heard your name. Every time you looked at me, it was on my lips to tell you the truth."

This seemed to satisfy Blaine as he visibly relaxed. They all moved to sit around the large kitchen table, Blaine in between

Justin and Rebecca, with Cordelia on the other side next to him.

When Cordelia had poured them all drinks again, Blaine spoke. "So, what do I call you? I can't very well call you 'Dad,' can I?"

Romilda chuckled. "No, I suppose you can't. It would confuse some people."

Cordelia held up her hand. "Can I make a suggestion? You can continue to call me 'Nan,' dear, as you've always done. You can call Romilda 'Mom,' if you'd like. She deserves some recognition as your parent. After all, it was me who kept her away for so long."

Blaine nodded. "Okay. So Mom...can you tell me what it was like? What you went through? I'd like to understand, even a little, if it's possible."

Chapter Seventy-Three

Everyone around the table visibly tensed. Romilda laughed. "Oh, relax everyone, curiosity is a wonderful thing, really it is. And it's a valid question. How else is Blaine going to get a true sense of my character?"

Romilda let out a deep breath and looked over at Cordelia. "Would you pour me a drink? This isn't a long tale, but it leaves me parched."

She waited until Cordelia poured her a glass of pink lemonade with a healthy helping of vodka. "Thank you, dear. Now, Blaine, you wanted to know what led me to my decision to transition?"

"Yes, if you can. I'm just trying to make sense of why you left, why you did what you did. I'm just trying to understand. I hope I'm not prying."

"You are, dear boy, but, as I said before, curiosity is a healthy thing and should always be encouraged. Never be afraid to ask someone a question, even if you're afraid to hear the answer. That's how hearts are broken and mended, how heroes are born, how philosophers become."

"Do you always talk like this?" Rebecca asked. "You sound like a book."

"Then it's a mighty fine thing that I run the GLBTQ Library, wouldn't you say?"

Cordelia put a hand on Rebecca's arm. "Pay her no mind. She was like this as a man, too. Always had a thirst to know more."

"That I did. Also a healthy preoccupation, it should be noted." She turned back to Blaine. "Now, you wanted to know how I chose to become this way?"

"Yes. I'm just trying to understand you. I don't know a thing about you."

"Yet, I know a lot about you. You're kind and sincere. You're of sound mind and heart, otherwise Justin would never have looked twice at you. I've known him for a very long time and he's never taken a lover before."

"Are you related?"

"No, dear boy. Justin helped me when I was becoming myself, as it were. He gave me lessons on how to look like a woman. Seems I was making a mess of things when I came out of the closet, as it were. However, I'm getting ahead of myself. You want to hear about why I left you and Cordelia, I'd imagine."

Romilda took a sip of her pink lemonade and made a face. "Dear Lord woman, how much did you put in there? That'll put hair on my chest and that will never do!" She took another sip anyway.

"Blaine, you have to understand something up front: I had no idea you existed until you were close to nine years old. You had started asking questions about your father and Cordelia thought it was time I met you. You're the spitting image of me when I was a boy, I see so much of myself in you and it's been a pleasure to see you growing up, even from a distance."

"Nan didn't tell you?"

"No. She didn't. Don't be angry with your mother; I broke her heart. When hearts are broken, they are liable to do some pretty horrible things until they find themselves again. But my heart was breaking, too. Being true to myself was the hardest thing I have ever had to do. Leaving your mother came second."

She took another sip of her lemonade. "That's easier to drink the more I have of it." She gave Cordelia a grin.

"When did you know?" Blaine asked.

"That I was a woman trapped in a man's body? Is that what you mean?"

"Yes."

"Why, always, dear boy. Always."

Chapter Seventy-Four

"You see, it was a different time back then. I was a different person back then," Romilda began.

"Yeah, for one thing, you were a man," Rebecca said.

Cordelia shushed her, but Romilda held her hand up. "She's right, dear, just a little bit more blunt than I would have been, is all."

"Did you always feel like a woman trapped in a man's body?" Blaine asked.

"Ever since I could remember. I thought I was gay at first, but I realized that I liked dressing up in woman's clothes because I felt more comfortable, more myself, not because I was gay."

"It must have been frightening for you," Justin said.

"Oh, it was. There were a many transgender people at that time, but no one I could talk to. They were all closeted or they isolated themselves. I did what was expected of me and dated women. When I met Cordelia, I figured I could ignore the feelings inside of me and become the man I was supposed to."

Romilda looked over at Cordelia and saw that she had a few tears sliding down her cheek. Romilda wanted to reach out and wipe them away but didn't. Each person was allowed their own grief.

"Your mother enchanted me and, for a time, there was nothing to ignore. She was, and still is, everything I wanted in a partner. She was funny, caring, and delightful. We married, and, for a time, we were very happy."

"What happened?" Blaine asked quietly.

"Well, what do you think, dear boy? I couldn't ignore who I was, who I was born to be, any longer. I started doing some research about where to go, who to talk to. Your mother never knew anything about this, of course. When I finally made the decision, I was nearing forty. I had lived a lie an entire lifetime long and couldn't do it any longer. When I told Cordy what I was doing, what I had to do, it was the last time I spoke to her. She cried for an hour and screamed at me, yelled at me. Then I left. I went to Montreal the next day and began my new life. I left a man but came back a woman."

Romilda took Blaine's hand. "You have to know I would have never left your mother if I'd known she was pregnant. I would have stuck by her, and by you, regardless of my feelings, and done right by you."

"I know that," Blaine said. "I know you would have."

Cordelia was crying openly now. "I'm sorry. I'm so sorry, Romilda, I should have told you when I found out. But it felt like you had left a piece of yourself behind and having a child mended some of my broken heart."

"Now, now, Cordy, calm yourself. I don't blame you for what you did or didn't do. That's all in the past. I only hope that Blaine can forgive me and we can start being a real family."

Cordelia sniffled and rubbed her nose with a tissue. "I'd like that very much."

"Wait, I have a question," Rebecca said.

"What is it, dear?" Romilda asked her.

"You said you married Cordelia... you never mentioned you got a divorce."

"Well, no, we never did get a divorce. But I left one person and came back as another."

"So? Your marriage is still legally binding, isn't it? What does becoming a woman change?"

"Everything," Romilda replied.

"Not in the eyes of the law, it doesn't. You never divorced, right?"

"What is it you're trying to say?"

"Isn't it obvious? You're still married," Rebecca said. She smiled, "I think that's kind of wonderful, don't you?"

Romilda was about to respond when the door opened. Nancy and Mike came into Nan's house and looked at all of them sitting around the kitchen table.

"Hey everyone! What did we miss?"

Chapter Seventy-Five

Mike was despondent.

After Blaine had filled him and Nancy in on what had been said that evening, he had gone home. Nancy had offered to let him stay at his place, but Mike had turned him down. He had to go home and find out how things stood with William, if they even had a future together.

He wasn't sure why he was so surprised or hurt. He had been expecting something like this to happen. In Michael's experience, just as everything was going well, that was when stuff when to shit.

It had happened when he was younger, with his parents. After months of fighting with each other, they had settled down and stopped fighting and Michael believed they were going to remain a family. Until his father moved out. One day he had gone out with his mother to shop for school clothes, and they had returned to find his father gone. He had left a note telling them he had fallen in love with another woman.

When he was in his teens and already out of the closet, he had fallen hard for his first boyfriend, sure they would have everlasting love... only to have that boyfriend go back to dating girls.

He was hurt and didn't know what to do, but that was a big part of his existence. Part of the reason he did so many drugs was because he felt so lost. He was lost within himself, lost in his day-to-day life. He didn't know how to find his way back.

Part of what had drawn Mike to William in the first place was that, for some reason, he felt he had found someone more lost than himself; despite this fact, Will had a way of guiding him back to himself, of giving him a touchstone, of showing Mike who he really was.

Mike had thought that their getting married in the first place would be the catalyst for their breaking up, but they hadn't. Sure, they talked to each other less than before, but neither was willing to say goodbye. Mike wondered if he was finally ready to say goodbye to William.

The mere thought of saying that final greeting to William tore him up inside. He wasn't sure what to do now, how they could move forward. Was this what love was? Was this what affection was?

He thought back to his string of boyfriends and wondered if he ever loved any of them, truly loved them. Mike didn't think so. He didn't know what love was until he met Will.

That didn't say much when they got together so they wouldn't be alone, but ended up sleeping with others. It just felt good to come home to someone, even though it was strictly platonic. It had been enough for Mike then; it wasn't enough for him now.

There was a knock at the apartment door. He had been half-hoping for it and half-dreading it. With heavy feet, he got up and went to the door and opened it to find William. "You didn't need to knock. You live here, you know."

"I wasn't sure I still did anymore."

"I'm not sure I want you to."

They looked at each other, took each other in. "So where do we go from here?" William asked.

"Well, you could come in. That could be a start."

"Yeah, but then you're going to want to know why that guy had his mouth around my cock and that'll make things awkward."

"Yeah, funny that." Mike walked away from William and

went to the kitchen to pour himself a drink. He didn't care what it was: whiskey, wine, beer. He just needed to numb himself a bit and to let his walls down. If he was going to talk to William, to tell him everything he was feeling, he had to be partially drunk to do it. He wasn't ashamed to admit that he was kind of a coward about being honest.

Mike heard William come into the kitchen behind him. "I thought I could do this."

"Do what?" Mike chose a bottle of whiskey. Less would get him drunk way quicker.

"I thought I loved you enough not to look at other men, not to want other men. I'm sorry, but that's the truth."

"Well, we all look."

"What?"

"Honey, I'm married, but I'm not dead. We all look. You have to decide if you want to fuck them, or fuck me."

"Why does it have to be so cut-and-dried?"

"Because I've had enough of sleeping around with other men. I want to sleep with my husband. I want to take the man I love to bed. But just because I love you doesn't mean I don't look. You know that, right?"

"Sure I do."

"All right then."

They were silent for a moment. Mike just listened to the sound of Will's breathing, and found his own breathing matching its pace. Finally, William spoke.

"So what happens now?"

"I think it's fairly obvious, don't you?"

William grinned and came towards him. "Do you want to be the top or bottom?"

Mike slapped his hand away. "That's not what I meant. What I meant was that I'm going to stay with Nan for a bit and give you some time to yourself, to figure out what you really want. You say you love me and want to marry me? Prove it."

Mike went into the bedroom to pack a bag and expected William to follow him. He wondered if William would give him an answer. When he didn't, when William didn't even stop him as he left the apartment, Mike knew what William's answer was, and his heart broke all over again.

Chapter Seventy-Six

Nan paced. She couldn't help it. She was too pent up.

Everything had gone so well with Blaine last night. He didn't hate her, didn't despise her for her secrets. Nan knew that she should feel lighter than air after having decades of secrets out in the open, but instead it made her more nervous.

She had been pacing since 6:30 that morning after only sleeping a few hours, and she was still pacing, wandering around aimlessly from room to room, but each room had things in it that reminded her of the life she had lied about for so long. The ornament that Blaine had made for her when he was a child that sat on her mantle that said 'World's Best Grandma' or the photos of him that she kept up in the library that showed him as a fresh faced young boy of twelve, unaware of the world he had come into and what it already hid from him.

Nan had even started drinking, and it was only eleven in the morning. It was a Mimosa, and that was considered a breakfast drink, but still.

She stopped pacing when she heard the front door open. "Nan? Are you home?"

Nan walked to the front hallway and stood with her hands on her hips. "That's a silly question to ask when the door is wide open."

"Well, you could have run out or hurt yourself. How was I to know? I was just trying to be polite."

Poppy shrugged and Nan was surprised by how much she wanted to smack her in the face. She took a deep breath and another sip of her Mimosa. "You're awfully brave, coming in here like this."

"I thought it would be okay. I mean, Blaine told me everything that happened. I'm sorry for putting my nose in where it didn't belong, but I didn't think you would tell him without a push."

"Honey, you didn't just give me a push, you pushed me out of the tree and I got wet from the baby's water."

Poppy gave her a quizzical look. "Say what?"

"It's a metaphor. I'm half-drunk and dead tired, work with me here."

"Do you have a drink for me?"

"If you're asking whether or not I have an alcoholic drink for you, the answer is no. I can give you orange juice."

"So says the woman who gave me vodka in my pink lemonade."

"I'm still a little bit pissed off at you, dear. And I'm an old woman. Age gives me the right to change my mind at a moment's notice."

Poppy grinned. "Oh, I can't wait until I'm that old."

"Oh honey, you're a woman, you can change your mind at any given time. Didn't you know that already? Come on in, I'll put a pot of bourbon on the stove. That's for me though. I'll find you something else to drink."

Poppy followed her to the kitchen. "I'm so glad you've forgiven me."

"Oh, now, let's not get too hasty. But yes, I have. Another grace of being my age is that sometimes it's better to let things go."

"Are you okay? You're pretty worked up."

"I'm just a mess about all of this. I mean, what if Blaine grows to hate me? He must hate me and the lies I've told him all his life."

"If he did, he would have told you." Poppy shrugged again.

"That's the way Blaine is. You know that. Then again, you raised him. "

"Yes, but we've never dealt with anything like this before."

"He's your son. You'll work this out. Don't you think we have enough going on without creating more drama?"

Nan let out a loud laugh. "I suppose I've been hanging around you lesbians and gay men too long! I'm becoming a drama queen! Now what's up dear? You didn't come by just for no reason. Let me make you a non-alcoholic Mimosa."

Chapter Seventy-Seven

Poppy waited until Nan had poured her Mimosa (really just a glass of orange juice, but still) to speak. "Nan... I wanted to talk to you about something."

Nan smiled at her. "Of course you do, dear. Why else would you come to me?"

"Your advice is not the only reason I come over."

"I know that, dear, you're family. You help your family when you can and that entails giving advice. Now tell me what's wrong?"

"Nothing's wrong, not really."

"Something's bothering you though, isn't it?"

Poppy let out a loud sigh. "How is it you can read me so well?"

"Because I've known you for over ten years now. I can tell when something is on your mind. I remember when you were a teenager and you got this look of concentration on your face, as if you were working out how to say what you wanted to say. You've got that look on your face now."

"Am I that much of an open book?"

"Yes and no. But there are some things that are plain as day." Nan took a sip of her Mimosa. "Go on, spill."

"Well, I've met a woman..."

"Oooh, you waited long enough to mention that! Don't you know that I live vicariously through you?" She clinked glasses with Poppy's. "Good on you. So why the long face? Is she hideous?"

"No, she's beautiful. She's perfect and wonderful. Her name is Dava and she's super smart, incredibly funny, and it's like I met another part of myself in her."

219

"Oh, she sounds dreadful!" Nan laughed. "Poppy, dear, why do you look so worried? Does she like you?"

"Yes, she even defended me against Connie."

"What did Connie do?"

"Tried to take a swing at me in the bar."

"Humph! Never liked that woman. So she's brave to boot. What's the problem dear?"

"I'm starting to show." Poppy said, running her hands along her stomach. "I'm almost four months along and I've already started to show."

"Oh dear, you've got nothing bigger than a Buddha belly yet. Why all the anxiety?"

"Well, last night, we kissed. She was very gentle. I even felt that tingle you can get, do you know which one I mean?"

"As if someone is lighting the candle inside of you. That one?"

"Yes! I haven't felt that for so long, I was worried that it had gone completely."

"It's never gone entirely. All it takes is the right person to relight the flame."

Poppy was silent for a moment and considered what Nan had said. Finally she spoke, a little catch in her voice. "That's the most beautiful thing I've ever heard."

Nan let out another loud chuckle. "Oh dear, that's just the ramblings of an old woman. What has you so concerned about Dava? She obviously likes you and the feeling is mutual if your candle flame returned. What troubles you? "

"I'm pregnant!" Poppy cried.

"I hate to tell you, Poppy, but I already knew that."

"No, what I meant is that my body is already changing. I'll be fat and ugly before long and she won't want me. What woman wants another woman who's pregnant?"

Nan patted Poppy's hand. "You wait right there. I want to show you something."

She left the kitchen and returned a moment later holding a photo album. "Now I haven't shown many people this book of photos. I had a friend who was a photographer after Ernie left me. He took some photos of me and I want you to look at them and tell me what you see."

Nodding, Poppy took the album from Nan and she flipped it open. There in an old black and white photo was Nan, who was very pregnant. She sat looking at the camera with a huge smile on her face.

Poppy smiled just looking at the photo. She flipped through and saw more photos of Nan looking gorgeous. "You look so happy."

"My friend had a way of bringing out the best in me. He was the only other man I ever loved. We lost touch soon after those photos were taken."

"Have you ever tried looking for him?"

"What? Of course I have. He's probably forgotten all about me now anyways. Anyways, I wanted to show you how you look to others. There's something about carrying another life inside of you that brings out your internal beauty. I wanted you to have an idea of how beautiful you are to other people. Being pregnant will just intensify that effect. No wonder this Dava is crazy about you."

Poppy was surprised to find that she was crying. She wiped at the tears on her cheeks and thanked Nan when she handed her a Kleenex. "I'm sorry, I'm getting all blubbery and emotional."

"Nothing to be sorry about. It's an emotional time. You love yourself, Poppy Stone, the rest will work itself out."

Nodding, Poppy put her hand on the photo album. "Since you've been so kind to me, how about I return the favour?"

"With what dear?" Nan took a sip of her Mimosa.

"I'm going to help you find your mystery man."

Chapter Seventy-Eight

Looking at Poppy with her mouth wide open, Nan closed it and took a deep breath. Once she had done that, she said, "You have to be joking."

Poppy took a sip of her orange juice. "Why?"

"Because I'm an old lady. My loving days are over."

"Just because you can't make any babies any more doesn't mean you've forgotten how the equipment works."

Nan looked at her open-mouthed again. She was starting to feel like a fish. "Such a thing to say."

"This from the woman that told me I needed a bit of muff diving."

"Oh. I did say that, didn't I?" She let out a sigh. "Fair point then."

"Seriously, Nan, what's so shocking about that? Everyone deserves love."

"I'm too old, dear."

"It doesn't matter what age you are, love knows no limits. Or, has everything you've always told me been bullshit."

"I know better than to bullshit a bullshitter."

"Fine then, why doesn't it apply to you then? What makes you exempt from love?"

"I had my chance and he wanted a different life. He did give me Blaine, though, so there's that at least."

"Now who's sprouting bullshit."

"It's not bullshit, it's the truth."

"Only because you want it to be. Why do you think you only deserve one chance at love? What has you so afraid?"

"I am not afraid. I raised my boy on my own without any help from anyone. Many women in my shoes would have given him up for adoption."

"But what have you done for yourself?"

"I don't understand what you mean. I go out and get my hair done every two weeks, indulge in enough booze to kick start a mule, and buy too many books than is good for me."

"Those are all great, but what about your heart? Don't you deserve love? Why are you running away from it?"

"I'm not running away!" Nan found the volume of her voice alarming, but not as much as the tears that were now leaking from her eyes. She did nothing to wipe them away. Let the tears fall like diamonds on her skin. "I'm not running away." She said this more quietly.

"Then what's the problem?"

"I don't think he'll want me."

"Nan, if he fell in love with you while you were pregnant with another man's child, I'm sure that won't be a problem."

"But look at me!" The tears increased. "I'm an old, used up, husk of a woman. I've lived my life; he wouldn't want me the way I look now. "

"But would you want him?"

"What do you mean?"

"What, Nan, you think he hasn't aged a day? You still picture him as young and fresh as he used to be? Men age too, you know."

"Yes, but men want what's young and hot."

"No, they don't. Some men prefer what's otherwise known as a 'lady.' Plus, if he loved you as much as you think he did, he'll still see you as beautiful." Poppy put down her drink and took Nan's hands in hers. "Don't be afraid to love, Nan."

Nan sat there, wondering at the oddity of a young woman like Poppy giving her advice on love. Finally, she nodded. "All right. I'm game."

"Okay!" Poppy got up and came around the table to give her a hug. "That's the spirit. Now we just have to track him down!"

"That won't be a problem." Nan said. "I know exactly where he lives."

Chapter Seventy-Nine

Romilda was really nervous.

It had been her idea to have brunch with Blaine, but she had no idea he was going to accept the invitation. Romilda had assumed that Blaine would want more time to think things over. I mean, finding out you had a father after wondering your whole life was one thing. Finding out you had a father who was now a mother was another thing altogether.

In fact, Romilda was more nervous than when she went under the knife. She often told people that she was always a woman, that the doctors were just letting her real self out. Having her operation was not a frightening thing because it was part of her path to becoming herself.

Having a son had never been part of the deal.

She wasn't nervous because Blaine was a reminder of the life she had led before, who she had been previously. Romilda was nervous because, despite Blaine's forgiving attitude, she didn't forgive herself.

The door to the Roasted Cashew opened and sun poured in. There, amongst a halo of light, was Blaine. Smiling, he made his way toward her and embraced her in a hug. "Hey, Mom," Blaine said.

Romilda chuckled. "Hello Blaine, that's quite the greeting. A woman could get used to such treatment." She was surprised to find herself blushing.

"Of course, you're my mom. How else would I treat you?"

Romilda sat. "Well, truthfully, I am your father."

"No." Blaine shook his head. "You were my dad. Now you're my mom."

"What does that make Cordelia?"

"My mum."

"You make it sound very easy."

"What?"

Romilda motioned with her hand, made a big circle that encompassed both of them. "All of this. I'm still trying to wrap my head around it but you're so damn calm. You sure you're not high?"

"Oh, if I was, you'd know." Blaine smiled.

"Well, then how can you just... just be so calm? Are you not ruffled by all of this?"

Blaine shrugged. "It is what it is. I've waited my whole life to find out who my dad was. Now that I know, I don't want to waste another moment being an asshole about it."

A pulse of pride went through her. That she had had anything to do with making this forgiving, loving man was a miracle. "You do me an honour, dear boy, that I'm not sure I deserve, but I'll take it. Now to change the subject, where is the lovely Justin? I thought he would come with you today."

"Well, I did invite him but he said the first time should be between us. He said he's see us both later at the library anyways and not to be late, bonding or no."

Romilda chuckled. "That boy, such a kidder. Are you happy, Blaine?"

"Of course I am."

"No, are you happy with him? I know it's been a rather quick courtship, but you seem so content with each other."

Blaine thought for a moment and Romilda watched him. She marvelled at how his eyes sparkled, how his lips parted slightly in a soft happy sigh. She had never seen anyone look so absolutely in love and hoped that she would find the same someday.

"He's wonderful. He's everything I ever wanted in a lover.

He's smart and sincere, funny and genuine. Justin really loves me. I didn't think I'd ever find anyone like him, let alone that he would love me."

"I know you've been hurt." Romilda was silent for a moment after that but knew that they were both thinking of David. "You should know that Justin is one of the kindest men I have ever met and he loves you completely."

Blaine's cheeks turned pink. "I know." He took a sip of his water.

"But what I'd really like to know is, how is he in the sack?"

Blaine spit out his water in a big spray of droplets. "Oh my God, Mom!"

Romilda laughed. "Oh, youth today. Hey, I'm an old woman; I have to live vicariously through you!"

Chapter Eighty

"I just don't understand what happened," Mike said.

Nancy sipped his coffee and wished he could add some Irish whiskey to it, make it an Irish coffee. "Men happened. You know how they are. The moment you want to change what they think is a good situation, they start to freak out."

"I just don't get it. Why do they tell you one thing and then go and do something else?"

"Oh honey, they're just telling you what you want to hear, that's all. That's all they do."

"Do you even believe in love anymore?"

The question caught Nancy off guard. He hadn't thought of love, or the concept of love, for a while. "I suppose I do."

"You don't sound too convincing."

"No, I do. Of course I do. We have to believe in the possibility of love, don't we? That it can happen to us, too? Otherwise, what else is there?"

"How long were you single before Devon?"

Nancy blinked. "A lady never reveals her secrets."

"Well, you're a man, Nancy. So spill."

"Well, let's see, I think it's been about six or seven years."

"Seriously?"

"Yes. There have been a few rolls in the hay, but no one like Devon. How about you? Are you going to be okay?"

Mike thought about it for a moment before responding. "I think so."

"So what's up with you two? Are you done?"

Mike nodded. "I guess so. He changed his mind and wants to keep sleeping around. I want him. We're in quite a pickle."

Nancy snorted. "Nice choice of words."

Letting out a chuckle of his own, he said, "Entirely unintentional, I promise you. I just don't know how things got to be so different. We had a good thing going for a while."

"People change. If we remained the same all the time, life would get boring, don't you think?"

"I suppose," Mike said. "I should be more broken up about this. My marriage is ending."

"Oh come on, you knew that this was coming for a while, right? I mean, you had to know."

"Know what?"

"Your relationship was based on sex and convenience. You had to know that it wouldn't last. You had to know deep down, we all did."

"I thought we loved each other."

"There are all kinds of love, Michael. And like I said, love can change, it can grow, or it can wither. There's no telling when that will happen. But you can't mope around feeling sorry for lost love. Isn't there anyone else out there that you're attracted to?"

"Yeah…" Mike looked away from Nancy and felt the blush come out on his cheeks.

"Then you have to tell him. If you like him, he has a right to know."

"I don't think he has any idea that I like him in that way."

"What did I just say? Tell him!"

"Okay." Mike took a deep breath. "I like you, Nancy. As more than a friend. I have for a long time."

Nancy, about to take a sip of coffee, stopped with the mug halfway to his lips and stared at Mike with wide, brown eyes.

Chapter Eighty-One

William was still drunk.

He woke with a splitting headache. His mouth was filled with cotton balls. He must have really tied one on last night. He tried to move but was unsuccessful. He settled for just opening his eyes and looking around the room.

William wasn't in his own apartment. He didn't hear Michael moving around, but he did hear someone. He wondered who he had gone home with last night.

After Michael had left, William had tried to pretend that everything would work out, that everything would be okay. But their last conversation had been so final and he had waited for hours for Mike to come home. When he didn't, William knew he had probably screwed up the greatest thing he ever had.

Michael and he had been together for almost ten years. In gay years, that was like thirty. He couldn't believe he had thrown something away so easily because he was afraid. He'd been afraid of the love that had been growing inside of him, afraid of fucking things up. So he had gone and fucked things up before someone else did it for him.

His previous boyfriend, a man named Clyde, had told him that he was a walking mess. "You're not sure what you want out of life, but so sure you deserve everything, that you just take everything without looking and wondering about anyone else but yourself."

At the time, William had yelled at Clyde, had called him an asshole, told him that he knew exactly what he wanted and it didn't include him. However, upon further reflection, he thought that Clyde had had a point.

After it became clear that Michael wasn't coming home (and really, why should he?), there was little for William to do but go out and get wasted.

He admitted to himself that this was probably not the smartest course of action to take, but he was feeling sorry for himself, so fuck it. What was one beer?

Then the one beer had turned into two, and then three. There had been some shots off the bar as well. Then there had been the mixed drinks and other assorted cocktails. Then had come the cocaine in the toilets. After that, it was pretty much a blur.

He knew he had made out with lots of men last night, but he didn't remember going home with one. How out of it was he? Did he do anything he would regret?

Hell, the last thing he remembered was sitting in a bathroom stall, taking a bump, and crying about Michael. Then he had woken up here.

Looking down at himself, he saw that he had been really busy. He saw condom wrappers on the bed, so at least he had been careful, even if he had behaved like an idiot. He wondered who had been desperate enough to take him home? Surely he was an obvious mess? Who would want to tap that? Hell, he even grossed himself out.

William let out a sigh, and his whole body hurt. He heard someone moving around in the room outside and then heard the unmistakable sounds of coffee being made. A moment later, he smelled coffee. At least some of his prayers were being answered.

He got up and slowly, oh, so slowly, made his way out of the bedroom. He should have stopped to put some underwear on, but the thought of coffee and some aspirin kept him going.

William heard the clink of cups as he walked into the

kitchen. He saw man with long blond hair pouring out coffee. "I hope one of those is for me."

When the man turned, William was surprised by how familiar the man was. The blue eyes held no warmth, but the smile he gave William was charming.

"Hey sleepyhead. How did you sleep?"

"Fine, I guess. Not to be rude, but what's your name?"

"I should have tattooed it on you somewhere. David," He said. "My name's David."

Chapter Eighty-Two

Poppy stared at her cell phone. She had never really been one to sit around and wait for someone to call. Then again, that had never been a problem before. She fell in love, and into relationships, quickly. Hell, she had known Connie for two weeks and they had moved in together. Connie had stayed for three years before Poppy got tired of her.

She only hoped that Dava hadn't tired of her already. Sighing, Poppy sent Dava a text: *I had a great time with you the other night. Looking forward to seeing you again.*

Poppy prayed that didn't come off as being needy, but she hadn't heard boo from Dava since the other night they spent together. Every sign Dava had given had been that she was interested in her, but Poppy was no good at reading people anymore. She thought Dava was giving all the signs of attraction, but how was she to know?

Rather than sit and brood, she called Nan instead. If she couldn't have her love story, she would help someone else with theirs. Nan picked up on the second ring. "Hello?"

"Nan! I know just what we need to do!"

"Well, hello to you too, dear. Did we already have a phone call? Or do you just like to start in the middle of a conversation?"

"Humour me. So you know where your mystery man lives right?"

"Yes, I've always known."

"Okay, so what are you doing this afternoon?"

"Nothing, why?"

"Well, before you go after him, we're going to go make ourselves beautiful."

"Poppy, didn't I already tell you that you were beautiful? And you spent an afternoon telling me that I was gorgeous, or was that all poppycock?"

"No, it wasn't poppycock at all. But why not look your best when you go after him?"

"Poppy, dear, what are you talking about?"

"I'm talking about getting a makeover! A haircut, a facial, the works!"

"Oh, not for me, dear. I get my hair done every two weeks at the salon with Romilda. That's enough for me."

"But when was the last time you did something wild and out of the ordinary?"

"Last night when I put tomato juice in my beer. It was quite good."

"Nope, that won't do. I'm taking you out to be beautified! What are you doing today?"

"Oh, today is no good. I'm just at the halfway point in *The Thorn Birds*, can't put it down now."

"Nan, you must have read that book a million times!"

"Yes, but I notice something different each time I read it."

"No more excuses! I'm taking you out to a salon and then we're going to make you even more beautiful than you are now."

"All right, dear, if it will keep you off my back. I still don't see that it will do any good. I don't even know if Joe has found another woman. It might be all for nothing."

"You know where he lives but you don't know if he's in another relationship?" Poppy snorted. "I find that really hard to believe."

Nan sighed. "Fine, as far as I'm able to tell, he's still alone. But he might not want me dear; we didn't end on the best of terms."

"When he sees you, he'll want you. Count on it."

"Okay, dear, if you say so. How's your own love life going? Heard any more from the lovely Dava?"

Now it was Poppy's turn to let out a sigh. "Not a thing since the other night. She's probably forgotten all about me."

There was a knock at the door. "Oh, that's good timing. She heard us talking about her!" Nan said.

"I highly doubt it's her." She stood and made her way to the door. "I'll pick you up later this afternoon? I'll make the appointments, you don't have to do a thing."

"Sounds good, dear. If that is Dava, bring her along, okay? She has to be vetted."

Poppy let out another snort, said goodbye to Nan and went to the door. She opened it to find the biggest bouquet of roses standing there waiting for her. Dava peeked out from behind them, her eyes flashing behind her glasses.

"I hope this isn't too much. You told me that you had never received flowers. I hope this is okay?"

Poppy let out a small sound of pleasure, and then she was kissing Dava. The scent of the roses mingled with the scent of her and then there was only the taste of her as everything else faded away.

Chapter Eighty-Three

When Poppy broke the kiss, she was light-headed.

"Wow," Dava said. "I think I'm going to bring you flowers every time I come to see you."

"You are the flower."

"Well, I've been called a lot of things before, but never that."

"No, what I meant is that you're lovely and wonderful and you make my head spin."

"I hope it's more than your head."

"God, you make all of me spin."

"That's better."

Poppy kissed her again. When she pulled away, she said the first thing that she was thinking. "I could love you," she whispered.

Immediately, she thought she had said something wrong. Dava became still and quiet and just looked at Poppy. More than that, it was as if she were really seeing her. "I'm sorry, I'm sorry."

Poppy went to walk away from her, to cover her embarrassment, but Dava stopped her. "What are you sorry about?"

"I'm sorry. I just say whatever occurs to me. I'm sorry."

Dava came into Poppy's apartment and closed the door behind her. She set the vase on the kitchen counter. "You haven't known very much kindness in your life, have you?"

"What do you mean?"

"You reacted even though I haven't said anything, even though you never saw my reaction."

"You got all quiet, I spoke out of turn, I'm sorry, I just blab and whatever comes out comes out."

"There you go apologizing again. You don't have anything to apologize for."

"I don't?"

"No. I'm honoured that you could love me and I hope we're on our way to that."

"Really?" Poppy let out a breath she hadn't been aware that she was holding. "So I don't have to be sorry?"

"No." Dava came closer to her. She reached up and ran a thumb softly along Poppy's jaw. "Who hurt you?"

Poppy let out a small laugh. "Who hasn't? I spent so much of my time with Connie cowering and hiding, never saying what I wanted to. I don't know how to do anything else. I mean, fuck, I had sex with a man to feel a little bit of love, just for a moment, even if we did regret it right afterwards."

"Justin doesn't regret it and neither should you. You're creating a life and that's one of the most incredible things a woman can do. I should know; I have three boys myself."

"You must miss them."

"Oh yes, they're all grown now, but they'll always be my boys. They have families of their own but, regardless of who I'm with, I'll always be their mother. And you'll always be this little one's mother." Dava put a hand on Poppy's stomach and rubbed it gently.

Poppy let out a happy sigh, one of pure contentment. "Will you stay the night?"

"I would love to. What are we doing in the meantime?"

"Want to come to a salon and get our hair done? You can meet Nan."

"Another ex-flame?"

"Hardly, she's my friend Blaine's mother."

"Do you think she'll like me?"

"Are you kidding? She'll fucking love you."

And then she kissed Dava again, feeling that all was right with her world.

Chapter Eighty-Four

Nancy woke and was surprised by how content he felt, more than he had in years, truth be told. He stretched and felt something in the bed next to him move. A second later, an arm went around Nancy's stomach and pulled him closer.

Though Nancy wanted to run, though he wanted to bolt, he didn't. Instead, he nestled closer to Mike and felt oddly comfortable. Rather than hold everything back, he decided to speak his mind, to be upfront and honest from the get go. Sure, Mike had known him for years, but he had never really been honest with a man that he was attracted to.

"I didn't expect to get to third base with you right away. I thought we were just having coffee," he said with a grin.

"Well, you did ask for cream with your coffee. Who am I to deny you?"

Nancy slapped his arm. "Jackass."

"Yep. Do you regret what we did?"

"No." He shook his head. "No, I don't. It was the first time that someone has made love to me."

"Nancy, I hate to tell you this, but you're far from a virgin."

"I know that. But I meant what I said. It's the first time someone has made love to me. We didn't just fuck or get it on or get laid. You touched me, you touched every part of my body. I don't think I've ever experienced that."

"You've been sleeping with the wrong men. What have you experienced then?"

"Well, Devon was all about the climax, the cum shot. He didn't care about romance or taking it slowly. Sure he was a great lover, but I don't think he ever really saw me. I don't think we ever made love. We just fucked. "

"William was the same. The one time we slept together, it was just fucking. I wanted to make love and he treated me like I was another one of his tricks. I was so put off and so nervous that I couldn't come. I felt like a failure, getting everything I wanted and not being able to give him what he wanted."

Nancy turned to look into Mike's deep blue eyes. He almost lost himself in them. "What do you mean? It happens, the body isn't perfect."

"I know, but first he went on about how he obviously didn't do his duty because I didn't cum. Then he would act all pissed off about it." Mike let out a heavy sigh and tried to release William from his soul. He was ashamed to feel a tear sliding down his check.

Nancy was silent for a moment. Then he took one of Michael's hands and held it with two of his. "You loved him." He said softly.

"I did. I loved the man he was when I met him. But I stopped loving him when I saw that my heart didn't matter to him, only his cock mattered."

"Is it helping, talking about this with me?"

Nancy felt Mike shake his head. "Not really, no. I don't want to talk about what's in the past. I'd rather talk about the future and what has yet to come."

Nancy let out a small laugh. "That's pretty deep for someone who hasn't had coffee yet."

"Hey, I'm full of surprises."

Taking a deep breath, Nancy asked the question he was most curious about: "Why do you like me, Michael?"

Nancy felt Mike take a deep breath behind him. For a moment, their bodies were one as Mike's stomach pressed into his back. Nancy relished the feeling of having Mike so close. As Mike took his breath, Nancy breathed him in.

"What's not to like? You've always had this way of engaging with life, of finding the joy in it, regardless of the drama that was happening around you. You see the good in everyone and that type of kindness is rare. You're a diamond, Nancy."

"Oh, nothing so common, I hope! Why can't I be a nice sapphire or a moonstone?"

Mike laughed and then his mouth was on Nancy's, and Nancy had no choice but to lose himself in the kiss and everything it represented.

Chapter Eighty-Five

Chuck was in love with Sebastian. He knew this for a fact. What surprised him was how easy it was.

They had spent every night together since his drunken professions of love and what surprised him most was that, aside from their one fight, they hadn't fought again. It had been two weeks without a fight, without an argument, a personal record to be sure. And he loved spending the evenings doing nothing with him. Chuck was used to the eternal conquest, the endless chase. He wasn't used to spending so much time with one man. However, Sebastian was more than any man he had ever been with.

Perhaps this was because he had just fucked men and moved on, never letting himself get close to them, get to know them. He was gone before any emotional attachment could be established.

He had brought this up with Sebastian one night, while he prepared fish for dinner and Sebastian prepared salad. This was an odd event too, making a meal with a man! It gave him a heady feeling that they could talk and work together at the same time and he fell even more in love with Sebastian. Chuck felt so comfortable around him.

"Well, I've seen it all the time, really. Men moving from man to man. You're afraid, or you were, even though you had to get blind stinking drunk to come here."

"Liquid courage. What do you mean I was afraid? I'm not afraid."

"You were. Emotional attachments mean letting down your walls and letting someone in. You have to think about why you were afraid and why you're not now. What started it?

What happened?"

"Life happened. I just never found anyone I wanted to spend my life with until you."

Sebastian gave him a look of disbelief. "There must have been someone, somebody who you loved before me. I can't be the first one, otherwise, how would you know that you loved me?"

Grimacing, Chuck turned away from the fish and turned on the stove. He poured more wine. "There was one guy." He took a healthy swallow of wine. "I don't know if I can talk about him."

Sebastian came towards him and enfolded Chuck in his embrace. He smelled of sandalwood and smoke. "You can tell me, babe, I won't judge. Who was he?"

"I've never told anyone this."

"You can tell me."

Chuck knew this without a doubt. If there was anyone who wouldn't judge him, it was Sebastian. He took comfort from his scent and strength from his touch. "He was my first real boyfriend. Of course, I had fooled around, but Francis was the first person that I really loved. We met one night at a bar and hit it off right away. It was like there was no one else in the bar; we only had eyes for each other. Only problem, he was forty and I was nineteen."

"He had problems with the age difference."

"Not at first. At first, it was all bliss and happiness. I remember the day he asked me to be his boyfriend. I was over the moon that someone like him could want me. Then little cracks started appearing in the mirror. He became short with me, told me things like I was too young to understand this or I would understand that when I was older. The break up came suddenly and I wasn't prepared for it. There was no dwindling of affection, no fights. I knew something was up though. I kept asking him if he wanted to talk about what was bothering him, but he said he was fine, he was okay, why was I asking?"

The words came out in a rush, as if they were rushing to be free after being held in for so long. As if, now that he had started, they did not want to be bottled up anymore. Chuck continued.

"Then one night, I went to pick him up at work. He wasn't there. I phoned his place and his roommate, this woman named Joni, picked up and said, yes, he was there. Then she said something I wasn't expecting, 'I'm sorry.' I thought it was because Francis had left without me, but it wasn't that. I took the bus to his place and there he was, blocking the doorway to his apartment. He told me he thought he could do it, thought he could overlook the age difference, but then he couldn't any longer, that he deserved a man and not a boy and I deserved someone my own age."

He became aware that he was crying, sobbing out the words, and they were becoming difficult to say, each word laced with knives and needles. However, something else was happening, too. With each word he let out, he felt lighter, felt more himself than he had in a very long time.

"I left his place and walked towards the bus stop to go home. I remember Joni coming out, running to me. She didn't say anything, just wrapped me in a hug and kept saying 'I'm sorry, I'm sorry.' It was snowing and I remember how cold the snow was on my skin. I remember how hot my tears were and how Joni wiped them away. When I got home, I lay in my bedroom for three days. I couldn't speak to anyone without crying. After three days, I stopped crying. I also vowed that no one would ever hurt me like that again. I would never let a man care for me that deeply or care that deeply about another man, ever again. Never again, until I met you."

There was silence in the kitchen that rang as loudly as cymbals. Chuck finally looked at Sebastian. He didn't know what he had expected, but it wasn't this: tears had left track marks along Sebastian's face. His open eyes looked at him with admiration.

"I'm so grateful. Grateful for you and so thankful that Francis was too stupid to see what he had and let go."

He took Chuck's glass of wine and put it on the counter. Then Sebastian kissed him deeply and Chuck gave in to the kiss, feeling seventeen years lighter.

Chapter Eighty-Six

William was waiting for Michael.

He would make everything right, would make everything good again, would fix what he had done. They had too much history behind them, too much of their story already told. William had to believe that Michael would fix everything.

His ribs hurt and he was pretty sure that he was going to have a black eye come tomorrow. He had called Mike on his cell phone and left what must have been thirty messages, telling him to meet him at the apartment. He had been calling him for hours when Michael finally answered.

"What do you want?"

He sounded upset. Maybe he was still as broken up about the whole thing as he was. William let out a long breath. "I wanted to talk to you. I need to see you. I need to explain what happened."

"There's nothing really to explain. You said we were exclusive, you fucked around, we're done."

"Please Mikey, please. Can you just meet me at the apartment? Does everything we have together mean nothing?"

"Everything we had together, you mean."

"No, have, Michael, have. We can fix this, I know we can. I forgive you, you know. It's going to be okay."

There was silence on the other end of the phone. William wondered if Mike was so overcome with emotion at being forgiven that he didn't know what to say. Finally, Michael spoke. "I'll meet you at the apartment in half an hour."

Then he hung up and there was only silence.

William sped over to the apartment that they shared, the home they had together. He was breathing shallowly so as not to make his ribs hurt more. He had changed shirts when he had returned home to find that he already had bruises forming all the way up his ribs. David had been so angry when he had left this morning.

When William had realized who David was, he went about gathering his clothes and got dressed as quickly as he could, stammering out excuses. His head still throbbed from the night before and the world was spinning. When David had realized he was leaving, he became angry.

He had started punching him, kicking at him. It had been all that William could do to get out of there with his skin still on his body, so great was David's rage. One moment he had been fine and the next he had completely lost it.

William paced the apartment, knowing that Michael would make everything okay again, that it would be all right. It had to be. Michael would make everything better. William heard keys in the lock and ran to the door.

When it opened, Michael stepped into the apartment... followed closely by Nancy. William's feathers were immediately ruffled. "What's he doing here?"

"He came with me. Speak."

"What?"

"You wanted to talk. You have five minutes. So speak, tell me what you wanted to talk about."

William looked at Michael with a shocked expression. "Why are you talking to me this way?"

"Why not? It's the way you treated me, like garbage. How does it feel?"

"What have I done to upset you so much? We love each other."

"You have to be fucking kidding me. Are you serious?" Nancy said.

"You have no say in this," William said.

"The fuck I don't. Look, honey, you're a friend, but you, Sir, are a bit of an asshole. To stand there behaving like you didn't do anything wrong, like you don't know what you did."

"We had an open marriage."

"Only because Mike loved you so much that he was willing to do whatever you wanted to be with you. Then you changed your mind and decided you didn't want an open marriage and you wanted only him. But how long did that last? Three days? A week? The first moment you get upset, you go off and let another guy suck your cock."

"Nancy, please, I can speak for myself," Michael said. He turned to look at William. "What he said."

William put a hand to his heart. "We can work past that, Michael. What we have with each other is real. You have to make everything better, you always did."

"I've finally decided that I want someone who only wants me. I'm worth more than you were willing to give me. And for the record, I have nothing to be forgiven for. You, however, do."

"So then will you forgive me? Can we start over?"

Michael was silent for a moment before he took Nancy's hand and held on to it. "I already have."

Chapter Eighty-Seven

Staring at Nancy and Mike's linked hands, William reminded himself to stay calm. Getting angry would solve nothing. He could feel his temper rising, however, and took a few deep breaths.

"So, what's this then?" he asked. "Are you two fucking now?"

A look of pain crossed Michael's face and William was glad that he put it there. "William..."

"Don't you 'William' me. You replaced me. You put me out on the curb like garbage. I'm that replaceable to you, am I? I'm just nothing to you, then."

"William, please don't be like this. You knew this was coming, you had to have known."

"We were going to get *married*!" He tried to keep the shriek out of his voice, the pain this was causing him. He wasn't successful.

"We already are married. You just wanted the flashy show. God, I wanted you for so long and then you decide that you want me when *you're* ready? Talk about treating someone like garbage."

William was shocked. He had never thought of that. Still, glutton that he was, he asked, "What do you mean?"

Michael let go of Nancy's hand and ran his fingers through his hair in frustration. "Don't you remember how it was in the beginning? How happy I was when we met? I thought I had found a man who wanted what I wanted, fantastic sex with every man we could find. We got married and then something changed in me. I thought that a married couple should actually sleep *with* each other, *not* everyone else. I talked to you about it, but you said you were hypersexual, that you couldn't limit yourself to one man. I believed you, gave you everything you wanted even though a part of me died inside."

"I didn't know you felt that way." William said, his voice almost a whisper.

"Didn't you? The nights when you came home to find me nursing a drink, my cheeks covered in tears? You chose to look away rather than to ask me what was wrong. Eventually, I just accepted that this is the way things were going to be."

"If you were so fucking unhappy, why did you stay?"

"Because I loved you."

William heard the word *loved* instead of *love*. He chose not to comment on that.

"Sometimes, we love the ones that hurt us most," Nancy said.

William turned on him. "You shut the fuck up, this is a conversation between me and Michael."

"No, it's not. It's a conversation you wanted to have with him, but it's not going the way you thought it would, is it? He's not saying the right things, is he? Not staying to the script?"

His temper flared and he saw red. William lunged at Nancy, seeing him as everything that stood in between him and Michael. He grabbed for him, but Michael was there first, punching him in the stomach, hard.

"You leave him alone," Michael said, his blue-green eyes alive with a fire all their own. "You don't get to touch him, or me."

William crumpled then. He slid to the floor, all thought of the image he presented gone. "You were supposed to make everything better. You were supposed to love me like you always did."

"I can't. I'm worth more than you can give me." Michael's

voice was soft and free of anger.

Looking up at him, William let it spill out. "Michael, what am I supposed to do? I slept with David. He hurt me, God he hurt me." He pulled up his shirt to show him the bruises, hoping that this would move him to show some kind of compassion.

Instead, Michael shook his head. "I'm sorry, William. I really am. You've made your bed, now you have to lie in it."

He took something from his left hand and placed it in William's palm. It was the ring that he had given Michael when they had gotten married all those years ago. Michael put something else in his palm and the piece of metal made a soft clink as it hit the ring. It was the apartment key.

"I'll have someone contact you for my things."

Nancy opened the apartment door and Michael walked toward it. Before he slipped out of the apartment and out of William's life forever, he turned back to him. "Find love, William. Life is too short to spend it just fucking around."

Then he was gone, the door closing behind him. William stayed where he was, feeling as if a part of his heart had closed with it.

Chapter Eighty-Eight

Blaine was leaning against Justin, listening to his heartbeat.

Even the sound of it calmed him, centred him, somehow. It was as if he had found part of his heart he had been missing, only he hadn't known he had lost it. What had he done to deserve Justin's love? Almost from the moment they had met, Blaine had loved him, and to Blaine, that was the greatest gift.

"Earth to Blaine, calling Blaine, come back down to Earth please, the people here need your keen sense of fashion."

Shaking his head to clear his thoughts, Blaine sat up properly and looked at Justin. "Sorry, I was a little lost there."

"A little lost? I was talking for five minutes before I realized you weren't hearing a word I was saying."

"Sorry."

"Don't be sorry. What are you thinking about that has you so quiet?"

"Just how lucky I am to have found you. From the moment I walked into that library, my life has changed. I used to find pleasure in helping people over the phone, but now I can find pleasure with you."

"What, so you're a phone sex operator too?" Justin wiggled his eyebrows. "C'mon baby, talk dirty to me."

"I'm being serious here!"

"So am I!" Justin held up his arms when Blaine hit him with a pillow from the couch. "Okay, okay, I kid. Do you really not have any idea how wonderful you are? Haven't I shown you or told you enough?"

"I know."

"No, I want you to say it like you believe it, not like you're just agreeing with me. I know you love yourself, otherwise how could you have survived everything you have? That was more than just self-preservation. Walking away from David was an act of loving yourself. So say it."

"I do," Blaine began. "I love myself."

"Louder."

"I love myself!"

"Say it louder, Blaine! Scream it to the hills and reclaim your heart."

"I LOVE MYSELF!"

His cheeks were flushed and he didn't remember standing, but there he was, his chest heaving, staring down at Justin. Blaine stood there, looking down at him, and realized he had never loved anyone more.

"God, I love you."

In one swift movement, Blaine swooped down and crushed his lips to Justin's. He tried to communicate everything he was feeling into the kiss, the love, the passion. The fact that something within him was shining bright, like a star, where his heart should be. A star that Justin put there.

He pulled away from the kiss and sat down beside Justin again. "Sorry, I got carried away there for a moment."

"Don't apologize, Blaine. You never have to say you're sorry, unless you're a complete ass about something. But don't apologize for doing something because you were moved to do so. How do you feel?"

"I feel as if..." Blaine took a moment to get his words together. "As if you've given me the stars."

"You haven't seen anything yet."

"What do you mean?"

"Well, I was going to wait until later, but this seems as good a time as any."

Blaine watched in mounting terror and excitement as Justin got down on one knee. Reaching into his pocket, he pulled out a ring box covered in blue velvet. When he opened the box, Blaine was dazzled.

Nestled within the box was a silver band, covered in a dusting of diamonds. Blaine tried to find his breath but couldn't.

"Blaine, will you do me the honour of becoming my partner?"

Chapter Eighty-Nine

Nan didn't know what she was doing.

Getting her hair done to make herself pretty. She wasn't beautiful, but she wouldn't crack a mirror. She was pretty, she gave herself that much. She couldn't believe that she was making herself beautiful for Joe.

Goodness, she hadn't thought of him in years, not until she had shown Poppy the pictures. Well, that wasn't true, she had thought of him. Often. Now here she was, heading to a salon with Poppy and Dava. After the split with Ernest, Joe had been a comfort. But she had been unfair to him too, had cut him out of her life to focus on raising Blaine. She had never felt very good about that decision. The truth was, she missed him too much.

Poppy disturbed her reverie. "So how did you meet him?"

"What's that, dear?"

"Joe. How did you meet him?"

They walked down the street, all three of them. Poppy and Dava held hands. For a moment, Nan had this vision of them in some sort of lesbian version of *The Wizard of Oz*. Muffs, boxes, and dildos, oh my!

A smile crossed her lips. "I met him at a rock concert."

"Which concert?"

"The Rolling Stones."

Poppy and Dava stopped walking and stared at her open mouthed. "You like the Rolling Stones?" Dava asked. "You don't strike me as the type."

"Well, you don't look like a woman who enjoys muff diving."

Dava barked out a laugh. "Touché."

"What was it like when you met him?" Poppy asked.

"Well, rather odd to be honest. He saw me across the crowd and moved his way closer to me though out the concert. When he was finally next to me, he realized I was pregnant. You should have seen his face."

"Was he entranced? Was it love at first sight?"

"No, he thought I was with someone, as I was very obviously pregnant. He apologized and moved deeper into the crowd. By the time I caught up with him, he was outside having a cigarette. It was raining and I could hear the sounds of the Stones playing inside. I'll always remember the song."

"Which one was it? '(I Can't Get No) Satisfaction'?" asked Poppy.

"No, it was 'Miss You,'" Nan sighed happily and stopped walking. "I started trying to explain, saying I wasn't with anybody, that it had ended badly, and Joe nodded and said, 'Good, so he won't mind if I do this' and leaned forward to kiss me. When we broke the kiss, he stepped back and said 'I sure hope you'll give me the chance to miss you,' which I just found incredibly romantic."

They arrived at the hair salon. As they went inside, Poppy asked quietly: "So what happened? You were obviously in love with him."

"You're still in love with him," Dava said.

"You're very observant. Yes, I loved him then and I still do. Not a day goes by where I don't think of him. I pulled away though. It was after he took those photos, and I realized how much I loved him, more than I had ever loved Ernest. I was afraid and a little shattered. I wasn't ready, I really just wanted to go and hide, focus on my baby and healing my heart."

"But you always kept track of him?" Dava asked.

"He sent me a few letters when I cut it off. I always kept

track of where he was, and he never moved. He kept on doing what he was doing and taking his gorgeous photos."

"Well, then it's time you stop missing him and go and get him!" Poppy said. "Let's make ourselves pretty!"

"Honey, we're already beautiful. You meant to say 'even more fabulous' right?" Dava said, smiling.

Chapter Ninety

Chuck was filled with bliss.

Every time he woke up in the morning with Sebastian, he was in a good mood for the rest of the day. When they weren't together, Chuck could think of nothing but Sebastian. How could it be that one man filled his every waking moment? How could he have lived without him for so long and not known that Sebastian was waiting for him?

Perhaps he wasn't ready for him. No, there was no perhaps about it. He hadn't been ready, but now he was. Snuggling closer to Sebastian, Chuck drank in his smell, his warmth. He could hear the beat of his heart.

More than anything, Chuck was glad to be completely loved. Though they had known each other for a short time, it was as if he had known Sebastian for much longer. He couldn't picture his life without him now.

Chuck wondered idly if he had denied himself the chance to be with another man in this way because he was terrified of being hurt again as Francis had hurt him; but he hadn't wanted to actually know any of the men he fucked.

With Sebastian, it was different. Yes, he loved him, but it was more than that. It was as if he had been waiting his whole life to meet him. He snuggled even closer and was about to fall asleep again when Sebastian turned and kissed him.

"Morning, lover."

Hearing that come from Sebastian's lips and knowing that Sebastian meant him made Chuck go warm all over. The love he carried in him for Sebastian intensified until Chuck was sure he was glowing.

"Morning. Did you want me to get coffee?"

"Coffee can wait. This is better than coffee."

Sebastian shifted and kissed him softly, his lips full and supple. Chuck grew hard, he couldn't help himself. He was happy to feel that Sebastian was having the same reaction.

When Sebastian pulled away from the kiss, Chuck saw the serious look in his eyes. "What is it?"

"Well, I want to ask you something."

"Ask away."

"I want you to live with me."

Despite himself and the love he carried inside him for Sebastian, the glow dimmed a little bit in fear. "Move in with you?"

"Yes, I think it makes perfect sense. We're spending all our time together, at your place or at mine. Wouldn't it be easier if we were together?"

Despite himself, Chuck's chest started to feel as if a bull was sitting on it. He wondered if he was hyperventilating, or if he had heard wrong. Just to make sure he said, "Move in together?"

Sebastian sat up in bed and looked at him. "Chuck, you have nothing to worry about. We're pretty much living together now, aren't we? Why would doing it on a full-time basis be any different?"

Chuck said nothing, he didn't know if he could or should, didn't know what would come out of his mouth if he opened it. He took a deep breath and realized the feeling he had was not of a bull sitting on his chest. He was short of breath because his heart had grown so much bigger. His love for Sebastian encompassed all of him.

Looking worried, Sebastian took Chuck's hands in his own. "Please, say something. Please tell me how you feel."

Leaning forward, Chuck kissed Sebastian deeply. When

he pulled back, the worried look was gone from his face. "I would be honoured to live with you."

After a moment, he decided that it didn't matter. All they had was time.

Chapter Ninety-One

"Knock knock, Anne of Avon calling."

Rebecca knocked on Devon's door again and waited for him to answer. "Devon, I know you're in there. I can hear you moving around inside. I'm not deaf and I'm not going away until you fucking talk to me. I've left thirteen messages and it's been days! Open up!"

She heard shuffling on the other side of his door and knew he had made his way toward the door and was listening to every word she said. Still though, the door didn't open. She tried again.

"You can't sit in there alone forever. You wouldn't even let anyone take you back from the hospital! How does that make me feel, huh? You won't let anyone help you! You did this to yourself, you know!"

She heard the locks disengaging. That had done it; she had touched a sore spot. The door flew open and there stood Devon, all black and blue, casts on both legs and one arm, the rest of him bruised and cut and hurting.

Rebecca knew he was hurting, she could see it in his eyes. They were wider than they should have been and the blueness of them looked like glass. His black hair was all messed up and she wondered when he had last slept.

"Don't you dare say that. Don't you dare. This was done to me, I didn't ask for it."

"Whatever, I still stand by what I said. Now are you going to let me in, or are we going to stand here arguing in the hallway of your building?"

Turning, Devon muttered over his shoulder. "Come in then, if it'll shut you up."

"Oh, it most certainly won't. You ought to know me well enough by now."

She closed the door behind her and locked it. She put the chain across it just in case. There was no telling who would stop by in this part of the city. Given what had happened, she thought the safer, the better.

Devon shuffled into the kitchen and took a glass down from the cupboard. "I take it you want a glass of wine?"

"Honey, when have I not wanted one? Of course I want wine. But should you be drinking? What do they have you on?"

"Tons of shit. Pain killers, muscle relaxers, and time. I've got so much time."

"Poor little bear. You sit down and I'll pour the wine."

Devon shuffled to the living room and Rebecca poured two glasses of red wine. He was more than just messed up physically. He was hurting mentally and spiritually as well. She didn't know how someone like him, who filled up every minute of every hour, could just survive doing nothing. But she would change that.

She went into the living room and found him sitting on the couch, tears streaming down his face. Well, she thought, those meds must be strong shit. "Honey, what is it?"

"Rebecca, I ruined everything. I ruined it all! He won't ever talk to me again, I'm done hooking and I'm ruined! I really messed things up, haven't I?"

She put down the glasses of wine and put an arm around him, pulled him closer. "I take it you're talking about Nancy?"

"Yes, fucking Nancy! God, I loved him, Rebecca."

"I know you did, honey bear. I know you did."

"But I didn't treat him right. I really didn't. It's my fault he won't speak to me."

"You were pretty tasteless. Going off with a guy for money

when you had one offering to give you his heart for free."

"I was a complete shit."

"Yes, you were."

"Gee, thanks."

"Well, I'm not going to deny the truth, Devon. You want bullshit, you go see one of your other, shallow friends. You want the truth, you come see me."

"So what happens now?"

"Well, the next time a man tells you he loves you, or you fall in love with someone, you treat them like they're priceless. The next thing is that I'll be staying with you for a few days."

He sat up and looked at her. "What? Like hell you will."

"Like hell I won't. I don't want to hear another word about it. You can barely take care of yourself. I have a bag out in the hallway and I'm not going away. I'm going to stay until you get better and get some of that sparkle in your eyes. We're also going to look at want ads for you. You're done with hooking and we're going to find you a new job. Deal?"

Devon was silent for a moment. When he spoke, his voice was free from any anger or sadness. "I love you Rebecca."

"I know, honey bear. It's just too bad I don't have a dick, or we'd be all set!"

Chapter Ninety-Two

"I look ridiculous!" Nan said.

She was looking at her hair in the mirror. Gone were her locks that had grown white. Instead, her hair was now a light shade of silver with white streaks and highlights.

"No such thing," Poppy replied. Her own red hair had been cut into a light mane of curls with blond highlights. "You look fabulous, Nan."

"She's right. If I were a few years older..." Dava said. Dava's spiky tresses were dipped in hot pink and shades of purple, making her eyes sparkle even more.

"What, don't you go in for older women?" Poppy teased her.

"Oh, you two!" Nan found herself blushing. She touched her hands to her cheeks, amazed to find the smile there. "It really doesn't look horrible, does it?"

"Nope. You look beautiful Nan, years younger but still a woman of wisdom."

"Oh Poppy, honey, you should have stopped at beautiful. Wisdom implies age."

"Not necessarily. I myself have always been an old soul, even when I was a young child. You can learn knowledge, but you are born with wisdom."

Nan laughed and it was as if a bubble had popped within her, filling her with light. She was going to do this; she was going to see Joe again. "Girls, I'm so nervous! What will he think of me? Showing up without a call, without a word from me for so many years?"

"Well, you'll have to find out," Poppy replied. "But he probably knows where you are."

"Why do you say that?"

"Well, it fits, doesn't it? You've kept tabs on him all this time. Wouldn't he do the same, if the love was so strong between you two?"

"Oh, Poppy, do you really think so? That we've just been watching each other from afar all this time?"

"Sounds kind of romantic," Dava said.

"How do you figure that?"

"Well, you never stopped loving each other, never let your love die. But held on to it and each other all these years."

Nan just looked at her. "Poppy didn't tell me you were a writer."

Dava blushed. "Is it that obvious?"

"Oh honey, only a writer could come up with something so beautiful when a normal person would hear of me keeping tabs on him all this time and accuse me of being a stalker!" They laughed together until Poppy put her hand to her stomach.

"Are you all right dear?"

"Fine, Nature calls."

She excused herself, leaving Nan alone with Dava.

Nan wasn't sure what she wanted to say so just decided to see what came out instead. "It's good to see her so happy."

Dava smiled brightly. "I'm glad I make her that way."

"She brings out a light in you, too, I can see that. Poppy hasn't been happy for so long. That's why she ended up pregnant. Not that that is cause for alarm, it's really a cause for celebration, no matter how it came about." Nan paused. "You don't mind that she's pregnant?"

"No, I don't. I think Poppy is a blessing in my life and so is the baby, no matter how it came about."

"I want to know what your intentions with Poppy are."

Dava didn't even take a moment to hesitate. "I love her completely. Never have I met a woman so full of love and life. I want to love her and the baby and take care of them both. I want to keep making her happy."

Nan patted Dava's hands softly. "That's exactly what I wanted to hear, dear."

Poppy returned, still smiling. "What did I miss?"

"Not a thing," Dava said.

"We were just plotting a way to take over the world someday," Nan said.

"And start our own line of sex shops," Dava gave Poppy a wicked grin. "A lady's work is never done!"

Chapter Ninety Three

Nancy told himself not to be afraid.

He was just going to say it. He was just going to tell him. Michael had a right to know. He had a right to see. Mike was in the kitchen making brunch for the two of them, singing something in his dusky voice that sent shivers of pleasure up Nancy's spine.

Nancy clicked open the document he had been working on. He had received the edits back from the agent and had some things to fix, but it was finally happening. He wanted to share this all with Mike, he had to be the first person that Nancy told.

He looked at what he had written, went through a few pages of it. It wasn't the poetry he thought he would write but nonetheless, the words had power; at least the agent thought so. Nancy was nervous about Mike's reaction, about everyone's, but hoped that he would love it. He was in it, after all.

Mike came out carrying two portions of bacon and eggs and fruit on plates and set the plates on the other side of the dining room table. Looking at Nancy over the top of his laptop, Mike laughed. "You look so serious. What's up, babe?"

"I have something to tell you. It concerns you."

Mike gave him a concerned look and came around to the other side of the table. "Okay, now you have me worried. What's going on? Are you ill?"

"No, no, it's nothing like that. I'm okay. I have to show you something. I want you to read something that I've written."

"I will always read what you've written. You know I've always loved your poems and short stories."

Nancy got up and let Mike have the desk chair so he could read comfortably. Nancy held his breath while Mike read the first page. Nancy already knew the words by heart:

"So which one of you fuckers is going to pay for this beer?"

Blaine turned and faced them.

Nancy, the delightful one. He was also incredibly feminine. Fruity, if you will. "I can't," he said. "I just picked up a new MAC foundation and the new Britney CD." Nancy shrugged as if this should be common knowledge. "I'm fresh out."

Blaine looked at Chuck. He was always out for a good time. Blaine knew he'd have cash on him. But Chuck shook his head. "Sorry man," he grinned. "But I got me some K."

"What the hell is K?" Blaine asked.

"It's the new thing, apparently," Chuck said. He looked around and quietly took out a little baggie. "Gives you a whole on body buzz."

"It's cat tranquilizer," Mike said.

Blaine gagged. "Cat tranquilizer?" Blaine took a sip of his beer to clear the awful taste in his mouth. "Why do you do that to yourself?" Chuck was always trying out new drugs and never turned down an opportunity to experiment. He also had more money than God and the Pope put together. If you're going to live the lifestyle of an upper class queen, you gotta have the money.

"Well, it's all right," Mike said. "But it makes you feel really groggy afterwards. I tried some with a guy I met down at The Cabin." The Cabin was a *happening scene for the young to the middle-aged. It was also rumoured to have one of the best cruising bathrooms in the city.*

"What is this?" Mike's voice was quiet when he spoke.

"It's a novel. It's a novel based on all of us. There were parts of it that I had to make up because I can't see inside of everyone's bedroom. But after the shit happened with Devon, I sat down to write a story or a poem and this is what came out instead. They always say to write what I know, right? So this is what I know."

Mike read further and then turned to Nancy. "This is incredible."

"Really? You don't mind? You don't mind that you're in it, that William is? That's okay?"

"It's more than okay… I'm honoured."

"An agent already wants to shop the book around. I'm almost done the edits he wanted me to do and then I send it back to him."

"What happens then?"

"Then? Well, hopefully someone buys the book and it gets published."

"Nancy! Oh my God, that's incredible! I'll know a famous author!"

"I'm not famous yet, but I want to tell you something else. The book ends with you and me together. You're my happy ending, Michael."

Mike shook his head. "You're not my happy ending, Nancy."

Nancy drew in a shocked breath. "What? What do you

mean?"

"How can you be a happy ending when we're just at our beginning?"

A surge of warmth filled Nancy and he pulled Mike into his arms and kissed him for all it was worth. Whatever came, they would be together. That was all that mattered. He would have to let the story tell itself to see what happened.

Mike broke away from the kiss and went back into the kitchen. "Where are you going?"

"To get the orange juice and champagne in the fridge! This calls for a celebration! How about a Mimosa with our breakfast?"

"Oh, can I have an umbrella and a maraschino cherry in mine?"

"Of course!"

"Make my umbrella a pink one!"

End of Lust and Lemonade
The Lemonade Series Book One

Acknowledgements

Though a writer writes alone, there are many people I have to thank for the book you now hold in your hands. In no particular order, they are:

Dava, thank you for beta reading the whole book and being my own personal cheering section.

For my Wonder Parents, thank you for being so awesome and wonderful. The support you've given me has made it possible to reach for the stars.

To Caroline Fréchette and all the lovely people at Renaissance Press for taking a chance on this novel. You've helped bring the characters to life on the printed page, instead of just inside my head.

And for Michael. Thank you for giving me your heart. You have mine in return and I love you more than words can possibly say.

About the author

Jamieson has been writing since a young age when he realized he could be writing instead of paying attention in school. Since then, he has created many worlds in which to live his fantasies and live out his dreams.

He is a Number One Best Selling Author (he likes to tell people that a lot) and writes in many different genres. Jamieson is also an accomplished artist. He works in mixed media, charcoal and pastels. He is also something of an amateur photographer, a poet and graphic designer.

He currently lives in Ottawa Ontario Canada with his cat, Tula, who is fearless.

www.ingramcontent.com/pod-product-compliance
Lightning Source LLC
Chambersburg PA
CBHW070844250626
47159CB00003B/916